THE
ITALY
LETTERS

THE
ITALY
LETTERS

A

NOVEL

VI
KHI
NAO

MELVILLE HOUSE
BROOKLYN · LONDON

First published in 2024 by Melville House
Copyright © 2024 by Vi Khi Nao
All rights reserved
First Melville House Printing: June 2024

Melville House Publishing
46 John Street
Brooklyn, NY 11201

and

Melville House UK
Suite 2000
16/18 Woodford Road
London E7 0HA

mhpbooks.com
@melvillehouse

ISBN: 978-1-68589-130-5
ISBN: 978-1-68589-131-2 (eBook)

Library of Congress Control Number: 2024930550

Author photo by Scott Indermaur

Designed by Beste M. Doğan

Printed in the United States of America

10 9 8 7 6 5 4 3 2 1

A catalog record for this book is available
from the Library of Congress

for my mother, mẹ Ngà &
for Giovanna Coppola

THE
ITALY
LETTERS

**Las
Vegas**

I do not know if this friendship has an ending. If there is an end for us or if this is, this epistolary letter, a way of saying goodbye to a future early. As you already know I am in Vegas with my convalescent mother. My mother doesn't want to die slowly, but rather quickly, the way my mentor passed, in her sleep. My mentor's death wasn't a cat drowned in a pool of light. I do not believe her death was quick. She had an interior torturous sixty-seven-year-old life, which led me to believe that was how she formed her endless compassion and love for me so early. I am in Vegas. In the early morning, I wrote you and when you woke up you wrote back. You asked me in the early morning if I worked better at night. I told you that Vegas was gorgeous and that I worked well when no one was around. You told me that you wanted to see the desert. You said you had never been there. I surreptitiously wanted to invite you here, but the lips of my fingers wouldn't move. I have been indigent and I have been vulnerable and terrified in the last three years and I feel I don't have anything to offer you that you would want. Not being able to afford a bed, I had slept on the floor for months before and up to nearly the night of my interview at North Domina. If I invited you to Vegas, it would break my heart to ask you to sleep on the floor with me. I told you in the early morning when it was 7 a.m. your London time and 2 a.m. my time that you would love it here. It's dry. The mountain has silhouettes. And endless nothingness, depending on where you go. Death Valley is pretty close, I told you. It's very beautiful when it rains. The fog drapes the sun, draping the mountain here.

Most people hate Vegas, but I have fallen in love with it across time. For its bright light and its angels of darkness.

The fallen souls that bind their hopes to gambling. It's a city filled with sinners in their sincerity to be fallen. You told me that you loved how you can love a place over time. I told you how it took me awhile to fall in love with it. It was a slow love like Venice was for you. Taking its sweet time. New York was a head-over-heel experience for me. It was terrible, I said. And, here, I found out how you didn't like New York. I fell in love quickly with it and fell out of it just as quickly. And, soon, you will wake up to wash your face, to attend to your tea, and to start your day. It's nearly the end of my day. Although I didn't want to go, I told you I must go and hold Vegas in my arms. In case she slips away. And I am utterly homeless in my evanescence.

Yesterday, my mother in her endless hacking and nocturnal sweating that soaked through her pajamas turned on YouTube for me. She invited me to listen to this song called "Còn Yêu Em Mãi." It was about a Vietnamese soldier who has been captured by the Việt Cộng. My mother told me that the soldier was also a poet. He knew he would die in prison and he wrote this song in prison, a letter to his sweetheart explaining his departure from life. In case you would like to know this poet's name: Nguyễn Trung Cang. In the morning, my mother, in her whisper of a voice, begged me that if she passed away in her sleep, to please wash her face and put sunscreen on it to help wash away the ugliness that death had imprinted on her. And, so it would be respectable for others to mourn her. Knowing that my mother has had a hard, torturous life, I selfishly want my mother to live. Not because I believe in life or in existence or we should be here longer than we have to. But rather, I want her to live because there is so much I want to do for my mother. I want to accumulate all the wealth I can so I can give my mother the lighthearted, blithe, debt-free life she deserves. I have been pushing my books out into the world in hopes at least one will reinvent the memory of the public and shower me with the economic prosperity I could afford her. Five of my books have entered the public face, if you can call sales ranking on Amazon at two to five million as having a public face. But they're out there. My sixth will exit the womb into the air. Crying hopefully, hiccupping hopefully, and burping hopefully. Over Skype last night, I told Cherimoya, my friend in South Bend, that when this child enters the world it would be fragile and pneumonic and it would find its baby mouth coughing with febricity. I don't want my love for you to be some vacant, distant memory, Gatto.

I hope you do not see this letter as being one. I tell you that I drift all the time now. The interview took much out of me. You tell me that it must have been so hard to do that interview. I think perhaps I need to drift. You asked if I were angry. And you said that sometimes life loses its lustre for a while.

Today I learned about your ancestry. You are Italian. Your parents are from Napoli and everyone before them is from Napoli. You were born and raised in New York. Your mother is from an island and your father from the mainland. But your Neapolitan parents met each other on a bus in Newburgh, New York, in 1956. My parents' marriage was concocted through an arranged coordination. My father fell in love with my mother and my grandmother fell in love with my father and so my grandmother wanted my father to have my mother. I used to believe in arranged marriages. But I don't know any more especially since my mother did not love my father and found him unbearable and intolerable. In 1989, when I arrived to the United States, we were both ten as you pointed out. Nine to be accurate since my birthday came three months after my arrival. Your uncle in Italy had pigs. He was a butcher, you said. And you had a goat named Daisy. When I think of your goat, I will think of it as a flower. Here I discovered you have three master's degrees. You have one in Liberal Studies, another in Contemporary Art, and the last one in Museums, Galleries and Contemporary Culture. When you lived in Rome, you ate bread with ricotta cheese and some honey on top and drank tea. When I lived in Providence, my breakfast was a cup of rice and sautéed salmon in red sauce. A sauce my mother taught me how to nurture from scratch by using three very simple ingredients: sugar, salt, broth. In the early morning, when it was cold in London, in the forties, before you told me that after a disappointing job interview in which you drew a mustache on your face and sideburns and called yourself Joseph, I asked you how were your testicles today. To which you replied that they were translucent and enticing like two pieces of salmon caviar. The conversation of your testicles led me to think of my trans woman friend who told me that before she exits her apartment, she must make sure that she hasn't left her testicles and spectacles behind. It was this same trans friend who abandoned my friendship for eight years before agreeing to meet me again just a few days ago. It was this same trans friend who in order to read my book *Time Is Lost* purchased a new reading table and lamp. It was this same trans friend whose quasi partner had been tortured and left for dead in the middle of the desert by a serial killer. She survived and when the rescue team came to airlift her to Europe where her father, who was in the Air Force, could provide superior care for her. It was this same trans friend who told me to pay attention to her partner's existence. Particularly to her partner's face which endured numerous plastic surgeries from the hammer blow by the serial killer, and to her feet, which were twisted, curled, and warped from the torture. She was only fourteen years old then. It was the same morning in which I told you that the college where I interviewed had someone in mind already before I interviewed for the job. I told you that I am just a wallflower who just found out that is just a wallflower. But you convinced me that I was a cypress tree that was hard to miss and that I smelled good. I don't know if I smelled good, but I will imagine myself as you may have imagined me: evergreen, refulgent, tall and redolent and green and leaning. I told you that I spent a month on that interview. Only it didn't matter. The stars already knew each other. Knew each other's alignment. What I didn't tell you is that the university is doing an investigation on faculty misconduct. The faculty affairs specialist had spoken to Cherimoya. If the university discovers misconduct (and no doubt in my mind that the interview process was fair or honorable or impartial), the Department of English and the Creative Writing Department would get a slight slap on the wrist and a slight reminder, like a wink, or rather two or three winks, not to repeat such an uneven-handed deportment again. It's not like the university hires someone every day. At times like this, I think of the tennis players who must face each other during intense competition. Especially when a lineman and even the umpire himself miscalls an important, decisive shot. The opponent could expend all the energy fighting the umpire for that one point and lose his focus or continue to make the most of the next point. The sad part about this whole ordeal was that the director of the program was adamant and passionate about advocating for minority rights. She was just lip-mouthing an empty gesture. The department ended up hiring a white Princeton male. Most of the faculty is white. I have been meaning to ask you without wanting to ask you about the controversy behind the privilege of whiteness and since you are white, how do you feel about the attacks against your race? I think about these things now. I also didn't tell you that one of the students, after hearing the news of the Princeton dude being hired via Facebook, rushed home to cry.

I haven't spoken to you in a couple of days. Which is normal. Our interactions are varied. Sometimes for weeks and months we don't speak and one day, it all rushes out like water from a waterfall. I would see you online and I want to wave hello, but I don't. I think about you a lot. I think about your quotidian engagement with your husband. And, why urinals appeal to you. I think about my vulnerable letter on its way to you. My days are devoted to my mother. To running errands and making meals for her. I run most errands for my mother because I do not want my mother to die and I don't want to fill my heart to the brim with regret. I don't want to say that my love for my mother isn't born out of guilt. Yes, duty or obligation perhaps. In the bright afternoon of Vegas light, I made my mother mahi-mahi soup with freshly cut tomatoes and pineapples. I sprinkled hot chili flakes, which my mother recently brought back when she went to Iowa for the birth of my first niece, to spice up its sweetness. To round the taste up, I squeezed 2/3 of a whole lime. I concocted this sweet and sour soup outside, using an abandoned ironing table for the makeshift cooking surface.

It's almost midnight here and you are about to wake up into your London light. I think about you curling up into a ball, but perhaps you do not want to curl. I still grieve my friend; you advised that I needed to put my grief somewhere to feel better. After much contemplation, I still do not know where to put it. I have told you about him. The one who got married and I went to the wedding reception in late July in Madison. The one who I had to befriend his fiancée in order to speak to him because he would cease communicating with me. This decade-long friendship ended the day he met his wife-to-be. I would like to think that I am one of those people in the world who doesn't just randomly get cross without provocation.

Insomnia has befriended my mother intimately. My mother feared this intimacy as she found herself coughing up a bazaar in the middle of the night. She feared the cough has invited pneumonia and bronchitis into her body. My mother depicted her pain along the side of her ribs as some rats munching. There was nothing I could do for my mother, but urged her to go to the hospital. In the morning I took my mother to a Vietnamese urgent care on Rainbow Boulevard, about a thirty-minute drive from Henderson, passing through the heart of Las

Vegas. During her violent diurnal and nocturnal coughs, she must have pulled muscles along her ribs, muscles she had never used before in her life, I assumed, bruising her lungs like an Olympic athlete during one of their marathon trainings. The human is able to endure a lot. We have the ability to overcome anything. My mother, on her best suicidal note, thinks that certain things are not worth overcoming. For the past two or three or five weeks, my mother said that if God calls her name to return to earth, she would welcome it with all her heart.

The Vietnamese doctor, the one with the last name of Trần, wrote my mother three prescriptions. He told my mother that over-the-counter medicines such as Robitussin and Nyquil looked really pretty, but they are utterly useless. He prescribed her promethazine-codeine syrup. It's an antihistamine. Vegasians, not vegetable or vegan Asians, are experiencing an increased dosage of allergic reaction to the dusty wind, like mini pockets of dust storms. Everyone thinks they are coming down with the flu, but it's our nature to fight against nature. We sat waiting at the clinic for about three hours. On the way back from the clinic, my delirious mother stopped by Sprouts to buy thirty pounds of naval oranges. She told me how she loved the way oranges cleaned her gums and gave her fresh breath. She even told me that one of the Sprouts customers asked her if she was allowed to buy that many.

It's in the late afternoon, almost an hour before you fall asleep, I sit to write you. Half an hour ago, my mother told me, "Now, I inject myself with this kind of cocaine." She is fast asleep with cough syrup and soon you will join her in her dreamscape, just thousands of miles away. I imagine you both, swaying in your soporific vessels in your separate hemispheres, while my mind slugs away like a snail. Earlier, you had written me. You told me that you got my letter and how you carried it with you to your job interview. You told me that your heart was full with my words. You told me about your nice day with four women and a black dog and how they wanted to indulge in your poems. You told me that at one point, you got very scared. You wrote that you had a copy of the five-page job description. That you forgot that you had printed it out on scrap paper and on the back were some of your poems. And how one of the women was turning the pages and she started reading and you started to blush while touching your cheeks and laughing nervously and how she stopped reading and they laughed and how you got red because it was a poem about masturbating and your dead papa. After hearing of your wonderful news, I told you that I hope your dreams swim like a fish tonight as tomorrow the eclipse will greet you. I wanted to say goodbye to you earlier than I wanted to because I was too tired. My consciousness was melting and like in the letter I wrote you, I felt my existence was dissolving. I wanted to hear more about your job interview since I waited three whole days for it.

In your London morning, you wrote that a magazine had accepted your poem about your masturbation and your dead papa. We were celebrating or at least I was celebrating it quietly for you. You also wrote that you had a dream of me last night. In the dream, I was an artist and writer and I had an exhibition and I was there and you were there too and it was almost like we were looking for each other, but never quite catching each other. I had objects in glass vitrines, books and things and sometimes someone would throw down some books on top of us from a balcony and you were trying to get a book of mine, but Herman Ham kept on getting them before you. Herman's an annoying guy and artist in London and he annoys you so much that you like him and tease him and at any rate, he kept on getting my books before you, which annoyed you, but it was good because it meant that he would tell others about me.

In your early London morning, before you fell asleep, you had reconnected with an old lover. When you lived in Mexico City, you made a bunch of friends who worked for United Airlines and they were lovely and they let you participate in their gay hedonistic mayhem. You didn't break up with your old love because they were casual midnight meetings and then when you left the country you didn't tell him that you were in love with him and he was also falling in love with you, but he didn't tell you either. You told me that you have tried casual sex, but most of the time you end up falling in love unless you hate the person. I realized that you fall in love easily and I hardly fall in love anymore.

My love life has been quite confusing. Suddenly, my mother woke up screaming from pain. I rushed into her room to find her sitting up, moaning. She whispered to me that this pain was more painful than childbirth. I offered my mother water while in the back of my consciousness, I am thinking that you had to start your day and that you had to go to the Algerian coffee shop to buy some beans.

Not long ago, my mother fell out of bed, landing on

the floor in her thoracic distress and torment. I did not know if my mother would get up or if she wanted to get up. I told her that she could sit there as long as she felt necessary. I told her that she had all her life ahead of her. I gave her my hands and I pulled her up from her thoracic slump and she was walking again like a crumpled piece of paper. In the crumpled state, she promised me that when she got better she would ask all her suitors on OkCupid and outside of OkCupid to buy my books and promote them.

Ever since I started opening myself up to you, my sex drive has increased drastically. I find myself constantly throbbing with desire. My breasts are engorged and my skin is sensitive to light and caress. To the sylphlike movement of the wind. Like a glass of water sitting on an empty counter, I get stirred easily. I had imagined you in between my thighs. I had imagined you curling up to me. I had imagined you pulling me in your arms. I had imagined you eating me until I was in and out of ecstasy. I had imagined myself in various, slanted states of your embraces. I didn't have the heart to tell you all of this. I feared this would be the end of our friendship. And so, to elongate our existence, or my existence of you, I imagined that you were atomic, that you could split yourself into two or three or four selves. There was the self that you could devote entirely to your Italian husband. The self that itself devoted to me. The self that devoted itself to your poetry. Sometimes, I imagined all of your selves lining up against a lake and I could see all the reflections of the people you encountered dancing in the fluid surface, like rain. We would all rain down upon you.

In my early March missive, I had written to you that I have spent the last three years of my life closing doors to love, to romantic ardors, to friendships. When they do not work out, I close the doors quickly so that there would be no opportunities for reentry. I told you that I have not always been this way, but I love the person I am becoming even if it means having less books, less friends, less family.

Codeine, not the band, knocked my mother out. Before falling asleep, I had imagined that we were taking a long train ride through Italy. My body leaned into you and you leaned in to hold me. You gazed tenderly at me while the landscape behind you kept flickering like light coming out of a broken idiot box. You wrapped your full arms around me and we kissed. Your lips were full like a bowl of water and my face was a washcloth. I soaked you into me and the image of us sinking into an embrace traveled with the train through the desolation of my imagination.

Before falling asleep, my mother climbed out of bed, in her broken skeleton station of a body, and wailed her way toward the bathroom. I could hear her wailing through my earphones. Sitting on the toilet like a cave, trickling with urine and tears, my mother moaned to God to exonerate her from this torturous life. My mother's body had become a Catholic church where wailing and oblations were being made. On YouTube, I was in the middle of watching "The Unmaking of Jian Ghomeshi," the Iranian fallen talk host seraph of Q. Fearing the depth of my mother's pain, I sat stoically like an un-pushed syringe filled with my own wretched medicine. But eventually she came out and she wanted to know why I sat silently in the dark praying to the God of Technology.

We watched Jian Ghomeshi together. I told her that Ghomeshi was very adorable and very charming. I google-imaged his faces for my mother to scrutinize. Later in the bathroom, my mother told me that she had encountered sweeter men. There was a great sweetness to him: just simply look at his smile and his Middle Eastern cherubic cheeks. At three in the morning, I told her, tomorrow the judge would settle the verdict. What is your verdict?, my mother asked. I told her that because he had an intensely brilliant lawyer, he would be appointed not guilty. This Marie Henein had already pulled lies out of these women. I told her that I believed the women. That indeed, he serviced them broken ribs, punches, strangulation, and violent sex. However, the women's narrations were not truthful either and since the law preferred veracity, in the case of sexual assault without evidence, the women didn't shower the law with this great preference and they were doomed for legal disgrace. If they had been truthful about their encounters with Ghomeshi after he abused them, the law may have taken their sides.

In the eyes of others, Jian Ghomeshi's sexual preference appeared perverse, but I think his taste was like everyone else's in the world. Except his was exposed to the public eye. If he hadn't acquired great fame and notoriety, he may not have had that many opportunities to exercise his sexual taste. Which is a fancy way of saying that his rise to power gave him proper power and more women to abuse. When women fall at our feet ready to be abused, we should take them, shouldn't we? We all fall from grace when our humility is lower than God. We fall from anything if we climb a mountain that God can't even climb. We fall from an empire we build if that empire is made from human skin and bones.

At six in the morning, my mother woke up from her codeine delirium to ask me about Ghomeshi. I told her, not until ten. I had also retold her about my dream. I dreamt of water and feces. Lots of water and clumps of feces in a cave. A huge wave came crashing. After a demonstration of needle and thread. For a book binding. The water came rushing and rushing. Most of the swimmers made it through the great water rush. But I remained dormant under water from March to August. Before emerging from the depth of water, I kept on asking everyone why I was able to stay underwater for so long. I kept on asking how did they know where to look for my un-submersion. Where to greet and retrieve me. One person disclosed that they came out each day to the same spot to wait for me. To wait for my re-emersion. My mother turned to me in her half-dazed consciousness to inform me that luck was heading my way. That my entire existence was a barrier of only good news. Parts of me thought that her rationality was fishy. A large part of me didn't believe it.

My mother and I then fell into a second wave of sleep.

When I woke, my body was swollen with desire for you and you had written me. You asked how I was and if I slept well. And I asked you the same. You told me that you slept so-so. In the early spring with changing light, you ended up waking up early. And, then you announced very quickly that you got your third interview and the job as marketing assistant was offered to you. You said that my words were a talisman. That you had read my poems on *The 2River View* before the first one. And then you read my letter before the second interview. And then you read my poems on *Plinth* before the third one. I then asked you what you wish to do in order to celebrate. You said that you were home alone and that you thought you would go to the city centre and smell some perfume. You wrote that this weekend you were going to make a cake and send me a picture of it. It was a cake your mother always made for Easter and that you have never made it. And, then, you added that you did not like cake. You said you never liked it and that it made you cook wheat berries, orange blossom water, and ricotta. Yesterday, you went to an Italian deli and bought these ingredients. The wheat berries came in a jar. My mother would be impressed, you told me. Then you quickly narrated that when you asked for the wheat berries at the deli the guy raised his eyes and said in Italian, "Are you going to make the pastiera napoletana?" And, of course, you said, "Yes." Your friend had depicted this whole thing like it was a car wash that you just had come out of. I asked you, "How is your car?" And you replied, "Blowdried and shiny."

When you informed me of your job offer, it was raining in London. I told you about once I showered naked in the rain. I didn't tell you the whole story, just that I did it once. It was at my mother's old house in Iowa City. The one she had a hard time selling for many years. Mostly, she left the house semi-abandoned once she moved completely to Las Vegas to start her dry-cleaning business. When I was in Kansas City, working for Citicorp, I had been accepted to Brown University and returned to Iowa City to live in her house to help her with rent and to make fast cash by scoring for Pearson reading essays, they paid per essay rather than per hour. Because I could grade five essays in an hour, this would allow me to make $60 an hour to save up for my move to Providence. The Midwest has always been known for its thunderstorms and at around midnight that one late summer, it thundered and rained massively. My ex invited me out to shower with her. With only one dimmed outdoor light stuck at the upper left corner of the basement door, my ex and I ran soap down our wet flesh. It was cold, not hypothermic cold. I remember the soap sticking to my palms and the hard surface of the concrete that trailed a walkway toward the outdoor parking lot. The shower felt scalding. I felt like a wet chicken dipped in a pot of boiling water. Luckily for us, my father, whose house resided nakedly next to my mother's, had flown back to Vietnam to make one of his impoverished women pregnant. Not on purpose, simply because he hated condoms and dastardly did not think a vasectomy was fitting for him. I couldn't afford my father the view of his naked daughter dripping in rain water from his backyard.

You were heading into the rain so that your body was a car and your eyes windshield wipers. I was still in bed, imagining you sleeping next to me. Ever since I opened up to you, my clitoris hasn't left me alone. I think often of our bodies as laundry sheets, taking turns folding in and out of each other. At other times, our bodies are linens, twisting, rubbing, slapping against the flat rocks and wooden slats made to remove stains and smells. In my mind, we would radiate on a watercourse and we would face portable washboards. We would be sitting on large watertight vats. We would be mangled, but still capable of compressing ourselves. We would stay away from yucca root and soaproot. We would sit out in the sun, waiting to dry ourselves in the wind.

Before you left our online interaction, you said you loved writing to me and that you would mail the letter you wrote me tomorrow. I wonder if you knew of my eros feelings for you, would you stop telling me things? I did not know if I wanted you to know. Perhaps this was something I could keep to myself. A secret between my mind and my body. For as long as I could. You didn't need to know that I desired you this way. It wouldn't help out our friendships at all.

When your letter arrives, I will be in LA to read from my poetry manuscript. My old roommate and former lover, Cherimoya, will be heading to the conference there as well and asked me last night if I found a sleeping arrangement. My ticket to LA, after points and credits from Southwest, costs only $1, or more accurately, 54 cents. But I couldn't afford a hotel stay and did not know where to donate my body. Through another friend, I learned that there was a free shuttle from the airport to the heart of LA.

I feared that with your new full-time job, your devotion to it, our interaction would decrease drastically. There were long periods when we didn't write or converse. There were long gazes into the unknown, where you made yourself a void and I was also a void. We had written each other profusely, it seemed to me, when I was in the affluent town of Tolland, Connecticut, where fog descended upon its population of fifteen thousands. It was that New England corridor that connected me to both Boston and Providence. I had written you while an artist genially and enthusiastically offered me a room in her condo to live for a couple of weeks. She had helped me evacuate from Wellfleet. I remember bringing my letter out into the snowy rain to take photos of it before sending it to you. And, then, you disappeared from view and for long periods of time, I wondered if we would ever write each other again. After my exit from Tolland, a poet and critic wrote and asked me, "Psychologically, what percentage of Asian are you?" By then, I had arrived into Iowa City, where the female gingko trees hadn't murdered each other yet using their ever-available spring-redolent artilleries.

Most of all, I don't expect my love for you to go anywhere, just to give me the optical illusion that there was time or the illusion of time or the illusion of knowing myself and knowing you through desiring you. Or the illusion of love. Or the illusion of desire. I don't expect you to leave your happy marriage. For you to become immortal or sapphic. Not too long ago, you had written that distance appealed to you. Perhaps it appealed to me too. We had connected more deeply because your mother has Alzheimer's and my love for my own mother was ever so abundant in its timing. I know you preferred men. I would prefer them too if their dicks didn't get in the way of me owning, I mean, knowing them. I don't expect these ardent pages to possess sporadic delirium, and, that over time, they would have the power to overtake me and conversely, overtake you. We are merely emotional seamstresses, tailoring our tailcoat of hebetude and vehement for any occasion. For our emotional outings into the modern world. I don't expect you to say goodbye just yet. Everyone wants their intuition to work for them, not against them.

Jian Ghomeshi has been exonerated from his sex crimes, I informed my mother. But his life is over, my mother exclaimed. The law has exculpated him, but not hoi polloi with their breasts exposed, their firm public face, their unshakable belief in their women, their protest signs, the company that hired him. My mother worried about his future. I assured her that Ghomeshi was going to be fine. He had money. He had that smile. He could spend the rest of his post–sexual assault days in the Bahamas. He didn't share the same fate as Oscar. In early January, I introduced her to the South African paralytic Olympian Oscar Pistorius. After looking at his picture, she declared, "This boy is so sweet, but he has undercurrent streaks of bad temper." I told her about Valentine's Day three years or so ago. About the bathroom. His lethal weapon. His beautiful, violent heart. His affluent uncle. His sweetheart. The fabricated intruder. The midnight air. Their foot fan. The two cellphones. Her modeling career. The small bathroom. Her preprepared speech against domestic violence and murder of women in South Africa on the day of her murder. The postapartheid condition there. The public bashing of the Black female presiding judge, Thokozile Masipa. The reversal of her ruling. The call for dolus eventualis. The nonexistent intruder who had to walk past their bedroom and use the bathroom before he robbed and murdered Reeva Steenkamp.

By morning, the day moved forward with alacrity and

my memory of it had become fuzzy. I had written you a note, reminding you once again of your job search success. This was before I learned that I had won the Toasted Coconut Innovative Fiction Prize for my manuscript with a provocative title, from Lawrence Zoet, whose email met my eyes at 3 a.m., reminded me once again that he had announced this news to me from Berlin. It wasn't like he was in the midst of his insomniac pose and felt compelled to write me in this fashion.

Later I wrote you, pondering if I should share this news with you, right at the feet of your success, but I felt that if I didn't share this with you, somehow you would feel slighted. Though, there would be no way for you to know about my omission. Considering that we had been sharing details of our doom and this was a shifting of a new light. I had contemplated whether to give you space for your success first before broadcasting the news to you. The more I thought about it, the more I felt I would cheat you emotionally of an opportunity to embrace my own micro success as well.

You wrote back, stating that you were engorged with happiness for me. Earlier you said that the rain had gone away. And that the post office was closed today because of the holiday weekend and that you won't be able to mail the letter to me until Tuesday. I told you that I was certain that your letter missed you and wanted to stay longer in London. You asked if my manuscript were another novel. I told you that it was a collection of short stories and a novella. And, then, my worry began to excite me. With your new job, I wasn't sure if you had time for my class. You simply said, "Yes!" Later, I told you that your success was contagious. It made me successful too.

When my mother heard news of my manuscript, she wasn't too excited. I could tell. She thought the prize money was dismal. I almost felt apologetic for winning it. But I felt it was better than nothing. After all, having only a few hundred in my bank account before my reading in LA invited violent feelings of desperation and ennui. With my mother on the verge of bankruptcy and her constant attachment to the stock market, $1.5K was a microsecond of profit in the great stock market exchange. I could see from her eyes that I had won basically a penny. What I had won would only cover living expenses for a month. This was the fifth year and the fifth time I had submitted to this prize and finally, persistence came through. What I had acquired across these seven arduous years of failure-driven submissions was not monetary based. Could my mother understand my wealth? When she had lost $200K within a year? What did I expect her to understand? My mother was under the impression that I would be poor forever. But I have a very strong drive otherwise. I wasn't going to die poor. Economically speaking.

Whenever my mother coughed, she exclaimed, "I can't believe you coughed for three whole months and you didn't say a word to me about it." I had been fighting something terrible and bad. Most likely it was acute bronchitis, the same thing that had attacked my mother. The truth was that I hardly told anyone about the torturous three months away from home when I coughed my chest out of my body. My roommate, Cherimoya, happened to know about it because she was my roommate and she had urged me to take medicine to mend my body, but I refused. For a decade, my body had been forced to endure the monthly doses of antibiotics to the buttocks, to prevent a strep infection from attacking my heart again. It broke my immune system and now, whenever someone became sick, I am the first to get it. I didn't tell my mother about my long illness, the violent coughing, about the surges of pain to my thoracic muscles after long days of coughing. I told my mother what good would it do if she knew about it. At one point in my illness, the coughing stopped. Cherimoya walked by my side in her nocturnal stroll to touch me. She had the false impression that I had passed away because I had stopped coughing.

When the surges of pain came to my mother sporadically throughout the day, I rushed to her side and informed her, "I understand and feel your pain because I had experienced it too, but you must endure it." These might seem like harsh words to my petite mother who had become green like an apple in the last two weeks where her body had been fighting this viscid thing. But no painkiller could offer my mother the visceral conditioning to want to experience life again. I wonder how you cope with your own mother. Do you ever talk to her shoes like they were old acquaintances? My mother's desire for sudden death had slowly become persuasive to me as well. I have come to terms that if I could choose to die, why not right now? Over the short time I had arrived in Las Vegas, my mother had convinced me that life wasn't worth extending. I agree with her now. Perhaps I had been agreeing with her all along. Perhaps there was the possibility of a dual suicide between a mother and her daughter. Between a seamstress and the writer. This was not a plot for a fiction story. Perhaps it was something one could experience empirically and not something I could write about.

And for the fourth day in a row, it seemed, my clitoris hadn't left me alone. It violently throbbed at the base of my womanhood. I am charged with this constant desire that felt systematic with the way the ovulation of the world works. In that, when changes came, they were unstoppable and the clitoris, or my clitoris, knew this too well.

Tomorrow you would bake a cake and you would show it to me in its digital form. I fantasized about what it would be like if you chose not to share that image with me and after this, we become distance, as if we hadn't ever known each other. I fantasized this because the possibility of losing you had become stronger and that statistics were against me. You were married and you lived in London. There was a part of me that wanted very much to abandon this friendship, to remove this desire I had for you, and to admit to myself that I had never known you. That you were just a figment of my imagination. You were not just a photon I held on to because I had been lonely for so long. You were not just a quantum of light that made me less desolate in the last week or so. You and all of your electromagnetic radiation in the form of a missive had kept me sane and wanted and desiring, not the world, but tenderness and love again. If my world hasn't been so thermal and optical, if my heart didn't have to swing between metals and semiconductors, if I hadn't been busy accelerating and decelerating, perhaps love would have been worth it. In my mind's eyes, nothing is worth it. I didn't want to tell you let's be subatomic or electrical together because how could we when we still use gasoline as our primary source of transportation. I didn't want to promise you anything while the entire content of my soul was obliterated.

I did wonder if my desire for you was born from a shift, a change, a transformation in me. That I had been dead for so long. I had been waiting for fresh air. For a fresh start. That lust, or the illusion of lust, or the call for lust was merely a symptom of that change and for me not to take it too personally or too much to heart. If all changes manifest sexual desires, love, then, I postulated, wasn't born from earth, but from the imagination. And if love wasn't born here, why, then, were we here?

There has been a light history in me, I'm noticing a pattern, of wanting or desiring married or attached women. I wonder why I preferred this kind of conditioning. It was something the least preferred. Or was it my preference not to culminate that I often found myself wanting and tending this garden of impossibility?

I had flown into Vegas to help my mother transition from one apartment to another and to convince her out of suicide. But it seemed the case had been reversed. I am convinced that death is better than this. Than this worn, war-torn life. In writing you across the board, I have applied as much sophrosyne as possible. From experience, friendships of this nature do not last very long. And, I don't know if I wanted to see the end of it, but I desired to at least say "hello" before saying "goodbye." In my mother's new apartment, carpet did not dominate most of the surface of the floor. It was vastly made up of pure dark, fake hardwood and her counter was marbled now. Her new apartment had new appliances such as the dishwasher, which we had been using daily, and even her microwave was fancier. This was to say that she had to pay $100 more a month for these new upgrades. The landlord did not want to spend another dime in her old apartment. He turned his dead ears upon us when we complained of the cabinet's veneer, which had already been peeling away and the hinges were broken, unfastened, and crooked. Mice were planting their small feces in newspaper and plastic bags. And, cockroaches as big as Tootsie Rolls nocturnally squatted openly on my mother's living room. Not wanting to invite disease and contamination by squashing them, I used to chase them with clear plastic cups and trap them in their new translucent domes. To prevent them from lifting up the domes, I placed *Crime and Punishment* and collections of love poems on top of the domes. In the morning, due to air deprivation, they lay dead with their spindly legs in the air as if begging sexually, "Please fuck me like a necrophiliac." "Oh, just fuck me," they seemed to say.

After waking up from a euphoria of codeine-induced sleep, my mother was sitting in front of the TV watching Annabel Langbein. My mother dragged me from the kitchen, in which I was busy making bánh xèo, to view the cooking show with her. This woman can cook, my mother exclaimed, and she used fresh, simple ingredients. We were watching her walk slowly and pastorally toward the goat, standing high in a wooden pen. Then my mother asked, like most mothers, "Why are the breasts of the goat so long?" I replied in Vietnamese, "Are you jealous that yours aren't that elongated?" "You know," my mother shared, "my exlover, that culinary one, used to milk two hundred to three hundred cows each morning. The cows used to look at him so kindly when he approached them. They had become familiar with him." Annabel Langbein walked back to her pastoral kitchen. She was carrying a metal milk jug with her and was in the process of making goat cheese. Seeing her placing a pot inside of a pot, a double boiler, I wanted to ask myself: Was the human embrace like this? The process of making cheese? When she placed the cheese into a brine saturated with two cups of whey, two cups of salt, and four cups of water, I knew human love wasn't meant to impregnate itself like this.

My mother's friend, I will call him Air Force One, invited us to dinner with him as a way to get my mother out of the house. March was considered the most beautiful month of the year in Las Vegas and my mother, steeped in her illness, was missing out on most of it. To entertain the possibility of exiting the apartment, my mother returned to bed for a long nap. I napped too. I struggled a bit because I was thinking of you. In your pre-Easter day in London. We had been communicating nearly every day across the digital plane and I didn't want to overwhelm myself with separation anxiety and discouraged myself from writing you or asking you how your day was. I wanted to see your cake and wondered about its adventure in the oven. I kept this all to myself. After my nap, and as promised, you showed me a picture of your orange blossom water cake. It turned out quite red and quite beautiful. You wanted to bake a cake to celebrate our recent success in the economical world, but perhaps also in celebration of our anti-doom. You told me that in the midst of making the cake, you thought of your mother and you listened to *Selected Shorts* and you listened to the Be Good Tanyas' album. It seemed the cake took you forever to make. It wasn't even your favorite cake. You spelled "favorite" with an added "u." How British of you. In reply, I told you that baking wasn't my expertise. Once I put a cup of salt instead of sugar and wondered why the house smelled so horrible. You also told me that baking wasn't your thing either, but the measuring and weighing calmed you. And, then out of nowhere it seemed, you asked, "If you were hungry and you had to choose between a slice of chocolate cake or a quinoa salad with pomegranate seeds and nuts, which would you choose?" I told you I preferred the latter. And, so would you. By then, it was almost midnight your London time. I asked you if you were going to turn into a squash soon. You corrected me by saying that you are turning into a zucchini flower. This image of you as a zucchini flower made me think of our common friend, Finch. She was still your friend, but when she deleted me from Facebook, we were no longer friends. But one of my favorite quotes from Finch was this: "I am easily forgettable. I am just flower and cleavage." Even you agreed that it was beautiful. And, like most things in life, you told me that your mom used to be afraid of her because she was bursting with wildness and freedom. Your mother was afraid that you would be like that too. You asked if I think I were wild and free. I told you that I believed in constraint. And you reminded me that we've talked about this before. I told you that a healthy bondage between leaping and incarceration produced great results. In December of last year you asked about traditions and beliefs. I had told you that constraint was quite a progressive thing. It was similar to thinking outside of the box. To be conservative would be not to act out of constraint, but to act out of rebellion and that conservatism inspired rebellion, which can lead to worse things. But constraint was a more mature version of freedom. It merely took utter discipline.

After letting you know that I would await whatever that was ready to spin out of you, even if it were not gold,

I left you in your digital plane to become the zucchini flower in your pajamas and I got ready to dine out with Mr. Air Force One and my mother. While we waited for my mother to get ready, Mr. Air Force One flipped through my book *The Old Cow and Her Sea* and immediately glanced up to tell me his opinions on the politics of transsexuality and how he preferred black-and-white laws to govern its existence. For instance, he preferred that if the transsexual male wished to keep his penis, he should only use the male public bathroom. All of these plumping problems could be easily overcome if we had unisex bathrooms. "I am not bothered," he informed me, "of a man wanting to go to a hospital to reconfigure his gender. He can be a woman all he likes, but if he kept his penis, he better not beg to play the female tournament at Wimbledon. It didn't seem fair. The muscles in his body haven't been downgraded to that of a female. She still possesses the strength of a man. She was still capable of hitting those one hundred and forty miles-per-hour serves." He immediately switched his narrative to the body as a weapon and in my mind's eyes, the human body has always been a gun, capable of doing violent things to others. We still did not have pistol control for the body.

We dined at Café 6 at the Palms Casino Resort. The parking lot was crowded. We didn't expect this pre-Easter Saturday to be filled with human fishmongers. We ended up parking on the roof of the Palms, where we could see the High Roller Ferris wheel. Here, Mr. Air Force One narrated an extraordinary tale of great veracity. A month ago, a Houston man by the name of Panzica was arrested for fucking, a one-night stand, a woman named Chloe Scordianos on this Ferris wheel which happened to be the same day he was planning to wed another woman. Several days ago, two men murdered him during a carjack. His wife-to-be was also in the car, but they did not eliminate her. They dumped Panzica on the side of the road and let his fiancée go. Scordianos did not add Panzica as a friend on Facebook. His death limited her chance. After all, she was one of the last few bodies who had the opportunity to understand his penis. On the ride back from our poor dining experience at Café 6, we continued to talk about Trump and what a travesty he was and how devastating it would be for our country if the United States elected this new Hitler to presidency. With his unspeakable rudeness, our diplomatic relations with other countries would be the least of our concerns. He had taken his penis to the podium. He had spoken of its size. Our military would be in great trouble if Trump decided to go to war using his human penis against North Korea's nuclear penis. It seemed so surreal to me. What is happening to this country? For the first time, America got to experience political candidates like it was Jerry Springer against *I Love Lucy*. Like a corn cricket fighting with an oyster. The incongruity baffled me to no end.

For most of today's afternoon, I have been thinking about you. In my mind's eye, I had been cupping your face with my hands. You were on your knees gazing up at me while I sat on a chair. Even during the drive to the resort, I thought of you. Your gaze remained concentrated and focused, displaying great devotion and loyalty and dedication as if you were delivering your entire self to me. It was this unerring gaze that eventually hijacked my clitoris to another state of utter fervor and compulsion. Even when I entered deep inside of myself, in which thinking of you brought me to here, I could not completely consummate my yearning for you. Even in my post-orgiastic state, I could not release all of it, this slow-building machine of craving and thirst. There had been at least four to five waves of orgasm and my urge for you remained still at its peak. How many orgasms would it take for me to come to you completely and utterly? In my landscape of concupiscent passion, you were on your knees, begging to eat me. You had been eating me all day, but by midafternoon, you wanted to eat me once more and once more again. The sincerity of your request and of my body's unwillingness to want anything else, I let you have me. You pulled off the curtain of my skirt. My pubic hair exposed. Your face pressed right into my circle of pleasure and ecstasy while you ate me eagerly and hungrily. Watching you eating me nearly drove me into another state of delirium. And, for an entire day we fucked nonstop. I could spend eternity thinking of you making love to me, of me cupping your face, of watching your devoted gaze fastened to my devoted gaze for you. I couldn't say I have ever desired anyone as much as I have desired you. Ever since you wrote that letter that opened me like a crack on the forest floor, I haven't been the same. If you had opened me up with your words like canned sardines, perhaps I wouldn't be here?

When I woke up this morning, there was a voice recording of you imitating your mother. I am happy to note that you should pursue a career in acting. Beneath your vocal performance, I noticed your great sense of playfulness and humor. And, beneath all of that human layering was loneliness. I had felt alone like that before, when I was straddling between the space between bliss and performance. I also enjoyed your high-octave voice. You also shared with me a picture of your pastiera napoletana sitting so acutely sumptuous next to your elegant bouquet of tulips. You had placed a mildly checkered cloth beneath the flower and cake. The display felt like a still life of Easter from the point of view of you. There was something pure about it. Not naked.

When I woke up this morning, my mother wanted to attend paschal mass. I had been trying to convince my mother during the last two years or so to attend mass, to re-ritualize her faith. With her descent into suicidal thinking, I thought prayers were the way to go. She finally decided she wanted to see Christ ascend to heaven. Wishful thinking of her own ascension into heaven as well? We had arrived to church late, but we lucked out and found a very good parking spot near the front. My mother claimed, "God must have noted that I have departed from him for so long that when I arrive today, He saves a sweet spot just devotedly for me." But when we entered the church, there were no more seats. I wonder where was God then? My mother and I ended up standing in the back, against the wall. One service man came toward us rudely and exclaimed that we couldn't stand there. Meanwhile other people were also exercising their spot at the back. My mother knew we were being discriminated. Leaning over, my mother told me to stay put. "We are not going anywhere and that man who was rude to us, well, he would have a terrible time finding a wife." Later, after we left church, my mother said that if she saw him on the street, she would spit on his face for mistreating us so poorly. Throughout mass, my mother was either sitting or squatting or standing. I knew her illness was still inside of her and I was secretly proud that my mother was exercising her faith. It gave me a little hope that my mother was going to be okay.

We talked briefly over the net. You and I. I asked why you were cranky when your cake turned out so tastefully. You were fighting a cold, you told me.

You also informed me that you had this strong desire to go to the store and buy a lipstick before it closed. But you don't really wear lipstick. I wonder where your intense, random urges were born. I told you about a dream I had of you. I didn't tell you it was a nightmare. In the dream, you were twenty-four years old and I was thirty-nine. I had booked an airplane to London to meet you. But it was sort of months ahead of its time. When we met, you hugged me and then you told me that I was old. I was too old to date. The dating part I didn't mention because I feared it would scare you away. You spoke to a man that we both knew in common at a big cathedral. And, when I met you, you did not look like you. You were wearing what most models in the design world were wearing: a black translucent drape. I had arrived by teleportation. Everyone thought I did not exist in that plane of reality, but you knew of my presence. Before I arrived, your space had been attacked by a bunch of animals. They made a mess of your space. So you chased after them with a frying pan. You were so brave. I knew I had committed the crime of omission by not disclosing the entire dream to you. I feared it foreboded what was to come between us. I feared that it was a sign that you did not want me and claiming that I was old was merely an excuse for such an omen. Eventually, I urged you to go for your phallic lipstick. You had purchased two cucumbers earlier after the wind blew off your hat and you had become cranky.

You told me that you were smiling big because you liked this dream. I let you enjoy it while I suffered a bit from the sin of omission. Then, when we conversed about my senescence, you told me how funny it was. While chopping vegetables for a salad today you wrote a letter to me in your head telling me how quite a few of your friends were older than you. You were telling me about your age difference. You said, "I was talking to you in your dream!"

I urged you to pursue your lipstick. I had woken up and I didn't know what the dream was supposed to mean. You told me that you kept on thinking about this hot pink lipstick. I urged you to catch your train. You wrote me that you were on the platform waiting for the train and I knew you were after what you wanted.

When I woke up I thought some more about Ghomeshi and the women he assaulted. I thought about the catch-22 of its law and logic. To hinge the acquittal on the veracity of the women seemed almost too psychologically exploitive and criminal-like. In order for the women to cope with their assaults, their minds must slice their memories into compartments that behaved like security vaults, ones that you encounter at banks. In order to function, they must cut some of their memories off. Even for me, when my mother asked me where I tossed the car keys, I told her a location. When she went to retrieve it, it wasn't there. Was I lying? Intentionally lying? I doubt it. And even for a nontraumatic event such as saying the whereabouts of the car keys, I had inadvertently lied without intending to. And, my mother didn't point a gun at me. It was only yesterday that I had a memory lapse. For the women of Ghomeshi to have lapses in memory about email correspondences over a decade ago, I could understand why the women were so sure that they had not contacted him after their assaults. I don't think memories behave like a series of numbers, but rather like an onion. One layer peeling off another layer until there was nothing left of the onion.

Many things faded, but not the assault. Many things fade, but we do not emotionally and physically forget how we are being treated. I rescinded my original stance on truth. Is it possible that in order for the truth to come out, one must neglect the truth intermittently? Is that possible that is how honesty works? When my ex abused me by throwing boiling phở at me, when she hit me, when she threatened to kill me, when she threw liquid detergent all over my head and face and my eyes burnt with utter agony, I stayed with her. She even made love to me afterward. I even brought her a gift or two for Valentines.

I even returned to the apartment after she violently kicked me out, leaving utterly helpless and destitute. I even hugged her and gave her a bath after she threatened to throw my life's work out of the window. I even cuddled next to her days after she threw a huge suitcase at me, bruising my thighs, because I didn't drive her to the airport like she had demanded. She stomped on my toes while I prevented her from carrying my laptop away in Las Vegas. I even slept next to her and told her I loved her after she threw a glass of water at my face during an argument. I stayed with her when she screamed for three straight hours because she felt I spent more time reading someone's manuscript than talking to her. The abuse went on for nearly two years. Was this my selective amnesia?

Sitting here, writing to you, I wondered if I would ever experience a healthy relationship. What it would be to know of such great exquisiteness. To experience it. Did I choose to remain single in the past few years because I could not trust myself to be in a decent relationship? It had become so utterly safe to turn to you for intimacy. An intimacy that had so much splendor, but also so much void. When men and women hit on me, I told them quite candidly to turn to somewhere else. I tried my best to immediately evacuate them from my existence. I de-romanticized their pursuits.

While baking a sheet of sweet potatoes, I thought excitedly of you. When I started baking it was nearly midnight my time and in London, you were about to wake up. I said good morning to you without telling you. Moments ago, I rubbed my hands all over the presliced bodies of the Covington, Carolina Ruby, and Beauregard. Every now and then, an image of intimacy flashed across my mind's theater. In it, you were leaning up against me. Your lips were just inches away. I cupped your face and kissed you. In that theater, we quickly moved from the chair to the floor. I was on top of you, making love to you passionately. My hands running between and beneath you. Could such level of intimacy and happiness and healthiness exist for me? Was it still possible as I was trying to channel my dream, my fantasy, my immortality through you? The point here was not to invite you to leave your husband, but for me to find my place in healthy desires. Is this healthy? Me fantasizing you this way? Or is this part of the cycle of heartache? What was my dream trying to tell me? That my heart was too old for you? Would I desire you this way if you were single? Then, I realized that when you went out to catch that train, you wouldn't be able to get your lipsticks because the store would be closed for Easter.

At one point, my ex had clarity. We were standing in my kitchen in Wickenden. Her back was to the light and I was standing in front of the light. I was in the middle of washing the white-painted floor with a coat of dishwashing soap. She turned to me, toward the light, in an argument in which I told her that the reason why she abused me was because she had been deeply abused herself and that I understood. She turned to me and told me with utter tenderness, "You shouldn't make excuses for the way I hurt you. You should hold me accountable for the way I mistreat you, Vi." She knew she was hurting me and she didn't have the emotional maturity to protect me from herself. She knew she was being abusive, but she didn't know how to end or stop it. It was one of the few times in my seemingly long relationship with her that I felt that she really truly loved me.

When I woke up, Mr. Buddha, who lived in Los Angeles, wrote me. He sent me a link to some conceptually compelling art pieces. In one, a headless woman pulls up the lining of her dress and a bouquet of light pink roses replaces her womanhood and pubic region. I immediately thought of you and of my protagonist, Ethos, who was courting his wife with daises and whom in workshops some readers, my peers at Brown University, thought he was too effeminate. I wrote you, "This is a great way to receive a bouquet of flowers." I thought my gesture had been too latently and overtly concupiscent and it may have offended you, but instead of apologizing or waiting patiently for your reply, I immediately fell asleep. Sleep solved all kinds of problems, I thought. When I woke up, I showed my mother the photo and she was appalled by its weirdness. "What an ugly thing," my mother exclaimed. I avoided my mother's repulsion for it by confronting what you had to tell me. You wrote back in response, "I'd love to deliver flowers like this." This is where if you had not been married and intentionally homosexual, I would have desired that delivery service to be me. I told you that the image was so aesthetically pleasing. I couldn't believe someone had taken a picture that was conceptually similar to my writing. You replied by asking me if I thought our thoughts travel in waves and somehow they make their way into other people. This question did not open itself to me until much later, when you were in your London bed sleeping deeply, and I had time to review our conversations for the day. I asked if you were feeling better. You told me that there was this cold that was standing at the door, but you haven't let it in yet. You were working from home all day on a lesson and then you went out to feed your friend's cat and you went to a store to get a notebook, but the store was closed. You got tired quickly. A man was walking two dogs and talking to a lady and he didn't notice the dogs were walking toward you and you couldn't get out of the way and you got tangled in their chains. Meanwhile you were listening to a reading of a story by Isaac Bashevis Singer while you were sleepily making soup. I told you that while I was composing an email to a publisher, I burnt the turkey patties. I apologized that you did not get your notebook and that I didn't have the heart to tell you that the lipstick store would be closed too. You told me that the stores were still closed today for the holiday. You confirmed that you went to get lipstick, but the store was closed so you wandered for a bit and it felt good to be out for you and by yourself and then you got tired. You told me about the story you were listening to. It was sad because it was a story about Jewish refugees and survivors in New York after the war and that it was an in-between world, between the past and future (the present?). I tried to look online for this story called "How High Deer Jump Son" by Stefan de la Garza. This story used to be free online. It is sad and beautiful and the story takes place in all time registers: past, present, future. I wanted it to couple with your Singer story. You were listening. I told you that I taught it in a class. It was a fiction class. I had seventeen students for the first one and six for the next. I told you that I had intentionally scared students from taking the class. You asked me how I scared them. You were picturing me with sharp teeth. I told the fifty students who were shopping for the class at Brown that they had to write two novels for the class. I told you that all of them dropped the class except six students. You assumed that they must have been the best students. I assured you otherwise. Only two out of my six students were worth mentioning. It was here that I learned your mother's birthday was today and she had turned eighty. Your mother had you when she was much older. She was forty-three years old and you were a surprise. I asked you, and not your mother of course, what it was like birthing you. You told me that you were a pain in the ass. That you had arrived early on the day that the new restaurant opened so she was in the hospital by herself and then you were born with pneumonia for nine days and you had to be in intensive care. Before you fell asleep, you told me that you read that sad story I recommended. You were one hell of a fast reader even if the weekend had made you stage yourself in limbo.

In the evening, I skyped with Cherimoya in a very small laundry room. She asked if I had a place to stay and when I told her no she half-jokingly teased me to have a one night stand every single day while I was in LA so that I could have a bed and some breakfast. She told me about the broken health care system, about her Madison friend who was suicidal and who had to admit himself into a mental ward and how he waited four hours in order for them to inform him that there may not be a bed for him since the hospital ward was overcrowded. I looked him up on Facebook and liked as many posts as possible in the hope that it would cheer him up if he fumbled upon it much later when he was down in life. Hoping that he wouldn't have annihilated himself before then. After leaving the conversation, I thought of you and the flower delivery system. My libido was like an opera singer. Her voice had been high and dramatic and I hadn't had the opportunity to muffle her. My body had become a pool of circular light, particularly near my clitoris. It was easily overwhelmed with even the slightest of changes in electromagnetic radiation. It was mainly all the time now that I experienced the length and width of my constantly evolving ecstasy. I wanted to know if the velocity of my desire existed in a vacuum or if you desired me too. You had asked me about wavelengths earlier. When I woke up, I had already desired you very much. My nipples, sensitive to only touch, no doubt they had become engorged with the ability to transmit sound memos, I thought. I woke up emaciated because I hadn't been eating enough. My mother wanted me to bake some turkey outside. Not understanding her intention fully, I took a frying pan out to fry the turkey patties for her. It was a disaster. I burnt the turkey and half of it fell to the ground. Outside, the wind had been whiplashing the trees back and forth, shaking the clinging leaves to the ground. It was a polluted day made of turbulent wind and pollen. I was outside in all of it, combatting the small gale while losing my breath. I was in the middle of writing to you while all of this was happening. Was it possible that you would reciprocate? Or did I desire so much that my mind was willing to bend sound and light?

I had been so hungry and then I was desiring you and my body was conflicted, between wanting to continue the conversation with you and nourishing my own body. When your words came through, my lower blood sugar level prevented me from carrying on and I ate. I made bánh xèo. I made sautéed rice noodles with spinach, asparagus, tomatoes, and French fries. I even had a donut, but I still felt deeply famished. My mother reminded me that I must have some meat to prevent me from feeling even weaker than I already had been feeling. I googled the high level of protein in spinach on the internet to assure her that my body knew what it was craving.

In the late afternoon, my mother's friend Air Force One stopped by to share with her his calculation of my mother's financial gains and losses in the past six months. He also gave us a bag of frozen catfish, tilapia, and swordfish. He also gave us a box of thirty slim cans of Michelob Ultra superior light beer. Because he used to work for the IRS, he will be filing my mother's income tax return for her. I think he will be spending the last two weeks pulling what is left of his hair on his nearly bald head in order to file the income tax return properly for her. With her gambling addiction in the stock market this year, my mother made over $1 million worth of transactions. Buying and selling and selling and buying. He told me that when there was a bold "W" next to her statement, it meant that she couldn't include those losses in her return and she may have to pay taxes on the gains she lost as well. These were wash sales and worthless stocks. I didn't have a clue on how he knew what column to comb through. My mother was too uneducated to understand all of this and she had proceeded blindly despite heavy warnings from her friend, Mr. IRS, also known as Mr. Air Force One. If my mother had to do her own income tax returns, perhaps she would think twice before involving herself in risky transactions. Sometimes I think my mother got away with too much and at times, I think life owed her big. I stood next to him in my mother's living room and I thought of his beautiful soul. He had already paid off his house and his car, but mortgaged his home so that his wife's family could build a big house probably worth about $150,000 to $200,000 US dollars in the Philippines. Now he was in debt and he thought he may lose his house because he could not make the big payments. I thought of his big heart. His big beautiful heart. How easily he was vulnerable to exploitation. I think of all the things I could do for him if I had money. For sure, I wanted to treat him to all the fancy meals and movies he had treated us to. One time, we went to Outback Steakhouse and the bill or the damage came out to be around $100 and he turned to me and declared, "Not bad." That evening when I climbed into bed, I thought of his teardrop-shaped gaze, his teardrop-shaped smile, and of his surprised expression of "Not bad!" My heart felt so heavy telling you all of this. He was my favorite person in Las Vegas. Mainly, I loved him for his kindness. I loved it when people were being kind. It made this world seem less barren for others, but also for me too. I noticed his arms more noticeably today. They were thin arms and filled with endless scabs, for all the falling down he had taken in the years he had become big and diabetic. If you didn't know about his history, you'd probably think he had just returned from the Iraq War. He used to be thin and a runner and I assumed athletic for his military training background. One time he fell down and shattered his toilet into pieces. I wondered if his body inadvertently fell and bruising came as a result and reminder of being beaten by his mother during his youth and of living in the same household where his father repeatedly raped his sisters. Did he become overtly corpulent, an extra layer of flesh, to protect him from this world? His body seemed like visual testimonies of his past and it seemed that the only way to know that he was alive and to have this unshakable past was to allow his body to reenter the unbreakable hemisphere of the ever-returning insulin injections, injuries, bruises, and accidents. But abuses of the mind and body were never an accident. They were part of the cycle of not knowing how to transform. He came today to share his movie collection with us. They were movies that tugged at the heart. One of them was *Notting Hill.* To lower his loneliness, I suggested to my mother that we should sometime watch these movies with him in our living room. We would have popcorn and Diet Cokes because he loved Diet Cokes. Of all the people in Las Vegas, I enjoyed his company the most. And, whether he had a crazy cat sister or whether he loved me like a daughter, it didn't matter. He was so kind. It broke my heart each time I thought about him being no longer in this world or in Las Vegas. Las Vegas would never be the same without him.

Before I climbed into bed, I thought of my clitoris as a flower blooming without my permission. Opening with provocation. Dismantling without justification. I thought: would you ever deliver yourself like that photo for me? Thinking about it now more concretely, perhaps just the thought of you delivering yourself that way was pleasure enough and it didn't have to have a future in manifestation. Sometimes desire peaked at its highest splendor from mere thought and provocation. Like lithography, it was purely in the lithographer's process and not the result, which was art itself.

In the early afternoon, my mother reminded me to rehearse. She asked me quite practically, "How are you going to perform if you are emaciated and you haven't practiced?" I didn't have a reply for her. I felt so doomed just thinking about my reading. It filled me with utter terror. I booked my flight to LA to launch my book. I was given five to eight minutes to read and I still did not know what to do with my body. Where will it sleep during its two nights there? With the unemployment office in Iowa accepting my form, I would have an expected income of three grand for three months. I worried that my potential two-night stay in LA would decimate it by 1/8.

It had been a wild day somewhat for me. I had driven down to Phở Saigon 8 to pick up phở bò viên for me cơm sườn nướng for my mother, but on the drive back I stopped abruptly at a red light and it launched the chè ba màu in the air and it landed on the empty passenger seat foot mat spilling part of the coconut cream, messing up the carpeted part of the car. When my mother sipped the phở broth and nibbled on the sautéed pork, her heart rate increased at an extraordinary level. She fumbled into bed to rest, to calm herself down. In bed, she turned to me and asked, "What would you do if I passed away? What will be the first thing you do?" Not wanting to prepare for her impending death, I told her that if she did die, I would wail. That was all I could do. I would wail. A fortune teller in Vietnam once looked into my mother's future and said that when my mother died, all four of her children would be present. I believed in this future so when my mother talked of nonsense such as death and suicide, I removed myself from believing her.

When I saw that a fellow writer from my publisher won the Whiting Award for nonfiction, I finally understood why I had been kicked aside to focus on his success. I understood why the reading was divided into three different parts. Why there was a separation between very successful, semi-successful, and little-successful people. To keep my head focus, to maintain my positive mental game, I read an article on Novak Djokovic, his transformation to becoming the Number 1. I can't prevent the Whiting

Award from awarding assholes who treated their students poorly, or North Domina offering a job to another asshole, who also mistreated the students. There is no way I have control over this, but I have control over my belief in myself. But I believe that my writing is at a whole different level than these people. That I can get there. If Djokovic was behind Nadal and Federer for so long and found his place in the world, I could get there just as easily. Part of my mind gets tired easily when I think about the future I can't control. A large part of me wants to evolve out of this. I believe I can get there.

When I woke up, you had written me. Last night, before going to bed, I had written you that if you wished to discuss Stefan de la Garza's "How High Deer Jump Son" to let me know. The following morning, you shared your composed notes with me. You told me that you woke up that morning with the story in your head. You had been thinking about it all day. You composed your notes in your notebook. You chronologized the story for me. You noted that three big things happened: 1) the boy's twelfth year birthday party; 2) the hunting trip; 3) the car accident. You noted that all three events didn't happen chronologically and he even died in the story from cancer and you asked, "What was it that pulled the story together?" You wrote that the narrator of the story was the boy-turned-man-turned-husband-turned-father, but the voice didn't change. He sounded like the twelve-year-old all the way through. You asked was it because that was the moment he came of age? The party where it housed his moment of public shame and the hunting trip, the moment of cover-up and lies? And the accident—the moment he was left alone, alone with shame, alone with a lie, alone with a daughter. You noted all of this. You even noted that the story was set up as if all these moments were side by side and that they work alongside one another. You wrote that time didn't mute them. That they were always there.

After returning home with takeout food from Phở Saigon 8, I looked all over for the story. I couldn't find it. I couldn't even find it on my computer. I told you that I read this story three years ago to teach it and that I needed to read it again to properly discuss it with you. I asked if you could send me your pdf. You had offered to give it to me last night, but I was too impulsive in my gesture. I sat myself down on the bed to read while my mother

calculated how I would respond if she were to die in front
of me. A messy pile of blanket and crooked pillows and
water bottles and computer and phone cords occupied the
landscape of my peripheral vision. I told you that after
half a dozen to a dozen times of reading this story, it remained as if it were the very first time. I asked you how
you felt about the story emotionally. You thought the
mother's slap was horrible and that you didn't see that
coming. You noted that the mother showed him shame. I
first read the story, I told you, in an apartment in Kansas
City. I thought the boy was trying too hard to be an adult.
He had imagined what love between adults ought to be
like based on his first hunting experience with his dad. As
I read more and more across time, time barriers, details of
his love life with Patricia made me think that he was telling the past from the future. Each time I read this story, I
discovered something new about it. That this was a story
that had five or six dimensions. All taking place without
me and later with me. You told me that you loved the narrator's voice. That it didn't change even when he talked
about himself when he was older. Then I learned that you
had read a John Updike story where he told the story of

himself when he was young and you could tell when he was talking about himself as an older man and when he was doing it as a teenager. You also mentioned the Eudora Welty story, which you wanted to reread now that you were older. You first read it when you were nineteen years old. The story had a title, "No Place for You, My Love." I asked you to tell me about it. You told me that it was about a man and woman. They went for a drive outside of New Orleans, to the coast, and there was a little dive bar and there was a jukebox. You thought they danced and then they drove back to New Orleans. That was it. They were not a couple. They each were married. And, you thought it was a story about a kiss that didn't happen. You thought that an older person would feel more than a younger person the impact of what didn't happen. I told you what I was trying to teach. I was trying to teach Ben Marcus's quote to my students: "One basic meaning of narrative, then: to create time where there was none. A fiction writer who tells stories is a maker of time. Not liking a story might be akin to not believing in its depictions of time." You were trying to picture this. How stories make time. Meanwhile I gave you a set of reasons to believe me. I wrote that what I think this story does so well—the image I have for it is—of a bread maker, a baker, using yeast to inflate it. One has the essence of dough. One has the essence of water. One has the essence of butter. And time, like yeast, inflates the bread of the narration. Now, too much yeast, well. And not enough yeast, well. One can expect not much to happen. In teaching this story, I wanted students to think about their ability to make time. Here, the narrator is utterly with us. Self-aware of his pain/shame/his devotion. Self-aware of his role in the story. You noticed that he also died and he was still with us. You observed that his pain or anger could have been overdone and how he could have judged his parents, his daughter, his wife, but instead he told us that his wrists hurt. That his face hurt or that he was cold and tired or the whiskey was strong. Then I added that I thought how his body was like a car. His father was steering him like a steering wheel. He was like a car that went through a car accident and he was narrating it from the point of view of the car. Then our conversation got caught on which characters lied and who told the least truth. I asked if you could reshape the ending, what would you like to convey. You imparted that you wanted them to respect the child without being condescending. I asked you what would you do if your child had an erection during his birthday party? You answered this. And then you asked me to expound on a comment I made earlier in which I declared that the father was single-minded about raising his son. He wanted his son to have a precise experience. The one he also gave to his older brother. The mother obviously did not approve. And indirectly, she did not show her support, though she did say to him to be careful. The least she could do since she gave up convincing her husband out of his stupid ritual, for good reasons. So that her son didn't experience the kind of violence that came from sex and death. The husband, being a father and not a mother, did not see this sexual death but it had been foreboding all along and proceeded with the game. The hunting. Until he taught himself his own lesson through his son. When he saw the violence of birth and death with his own eyes, when the father had to slice the mother deer/doe open to bury the fetus deer, it was an eye-opening experience, an awakening, for them both. The father coming of age. The son coming of age. The mother coming of age. You asked why did the mother slap him after his public erection shaming. I had replied that the mother slapped him because she didn't know any better. She didn't know that he had just killed a pregnant deer with his father. But you astutely observed that she slapped him because she didn't know how to make it stop. The public shaming. The un-erection of his penis. And, then I thought, if I had a son who had an erection in front of his peers, what would I do? Would slapping him be a compassionate way to allow him to exit the shame? Or was it to punish him publicly for the way he behaved? Or perhaps the situation could only be understood with a slap? I could imagine how painful this was for the mother to see her very own son being mocked by his peers. You observed that the slap showed to everyone that he was still a child and I added that an erection didn't purchase him his manhood. The same as drinking whisky or shooting deer, you added. And, then, you noted quite painfully that if you had had an erection, your mother would have slapped you. You noted that your mother would have been ashamed of you, ashamed of the sex and desire. She would have slapped you for making it public. In the end, you told me that you would be pushing your mother on a swing. I imagined the swing as pink as a peach. You helped me open my eyes to another layer into that Garza story, which I have read so many times. Before parting ways, before I told you that you must be on your way to becoming a zucchini flower, you thanked me for telling you about it. You were so excited to talk about it with me. The way the story got bigger and bigger. And as I predicted, you mailed the letter today, as you have promised. By then, I had wondered how you managed to stay abroad for eight years. This expat lifestyle. Your job offer made it concrete for you and that you felt that you could stay. It was grit, we discovered, that shaped our success in the things we did.

In the evening, my mother wanted to watch a movie. We watched *Notting Hill* and London was all over my face and so was the British accent. And, I think, what a coincidence.

I haven't been telling you about my clitoris today because it continued to have its own mind. It continued to throb. Later when I visited your blog on Italy, I noticed cooking recipes. I discovered that you thought about food all the time and I learned something new about you. You were hypoglycemic. Deficiencies of glucose in your bloodstream made you this way.

At the bankruptcy lawyer office, I noticed my mother's hands. Her hands were very beautiful, but my mother didn't think they were. She was always hiding her hands whenever I took photographs of her. These were hands that endured decades of hardship. Seeing her hands, they pained me like watching a deer get torn apart by the slow-moving bullets of time.

A panic state of mind sent me into another state of delirium.

Los
Angeles

I have returned from Los Angeles Convention Center. We have been out of communication for a few days and although I was unable to attach any emotional content to our correspondence during the previous week or so, the distance that existed between us made it impossible for me to listen to my clitoris the same way I had been listening to it before my trip to LA. When I took the red Metro into Hollywood/Vine, I thought about the theatrical theater of life. Rolls of unwritten tapes lapsed and got rewritten into our days. I thought of Cherimoya, my former roommate. She had become one of my favorite persons in the world. Although there was no corporeality or concupiscent dimension to my love for her, my tenderness toward her had become more and more profuse. I could say to you that I love her dearly. My love for her had become more mature and it overlapped into everything I did. Yet, when I stood on that Metro platform, I finally understood that my desire for you could not be compared with my love for her. I finally understood why all loves could not be compared to each other.

When Cherimoya greeted me at the lobby of the convention center and there had been a brief duration of one month in which I hadn't seen her, it felt to me that I was meeting a man dressed in a pink shirt and this man-woman occupied a large part of my platonic soul. But was it possible to fall in love with a friend without desiring her? Without wanting her in bed, but wanting to be close and intimate with her outside the bedchamber? Was it possible to love someone so dearly with the glamour of sex removed? Spending time with her was an absolute joy. A large part of it was due in part because she got irritable so easily. It made her charming and adorable in an

unpredictable way. She didn't want to take the Metro. I
had convinced her to take the Metro instead of an Uber or
taxi. It reduced the cost from $25 to $1.75 and she stood
there on the platform, in her semi-cantankerous impatient
way and my love for her augmented. In that platform, she
stood against the air like an angry twig. She had been the
one to introduce me to Angry Birds, though our relationship could not be compared to an addictive game made by
a famous Vietnamese game programmer.

We dined several times together. The second time was
at the Korean restaurant. She was craving kimbap. When
they served us kimbap, it was the Korean version of sushi.
She thought it was soup like phở. She over-ordered. She even
ordered fish ball soup. Our stomachs were tight like the taut
leather skin of the drum stretched to the maximum. The
host and server asked if we would like to take her kimbap
to go. I had packed it nicely for Cherimoya and in a rush to
get to my reading, we left it in the restaurant, sitting recalci-
trantly on the register counter. We almost missed my reading
at the Poetic Research Bureau in Chinatown. She thought
taking the taxi was the best way to get anywhere, but the taxi
driver did not know where to drop us off. We asked him to
drop us meters away from where we ought to be.

The first time was a long tedious walk from the convention to a disturbing phony phở place run by a Chinese woman in the food court, which also served tacos and chicken wings. The broth was Chinese made and seemed to have this thickness like the non-Vietnamese chef had added rice flour to thicken it or rather her beef broth tasted like chicken noodle soup. The faux phở was warm and Cherimoya was famished. I was also hungry myself. We originally ordered two, but she only accepted cash and I only had enough money for one bowl of broth. In her ravenous confusion, Cherimoya confused bean sprout for the phở noodle. I laughed at her esurient blunder. If I only had had several bites of cake and coffee for the entire day, at 5 p.m. I would have confused the lake for the sky or Jesus for Elmo.

The last day I was there, I met up with a publisher. Before we settled to talk, he told me he had to contort a pistol into a flower. I had heard that expression before, but in the context of us meeting up at a round table inside the book fair and with my mother speaking to me all the time in Vietnamese, language dislocated itself from my consciousness. I thought he had asked if we could stop here, in the middle of the book fair, to pee. I gazed at him, startled. Then, suddenly, he bifurcated paths with me, pushing his body toward the restroom sign. Relieved, I sat myself down. So that was what he meant. I counted my blessings that he did not decide to urinate here. I wouldn't have been able explain to the people at my table why I had left the book signing for urine exposure. It wasn't just anyone's urine. It was my publisher's urine.

After the piss stop, he asked me if I had questions. I had no questions. He asked me about a contest I had won. With poets, writers, and sycophants swirling behind him and around us, he thought it was a bad idea to flood the market with my books. Economically speaking, it was bad. Also, reviewers wouldn't like it. *The New York Times* wouldn't like it. He asked why I wanted to push my work into the world so rapidly. I gave him an answer I was terribly dissatisfied with. I told him in a slanted fashion that I wanted to get rid of them so I could produce more creative stuff. What I meant to say without revealing too much about my existence or my mother's existence was that my mother was suicidal and I wanted my book to economically explode so that I could give my mother the kind of retirement she desired. With my mother's quotidian mantra she rehashed every day about wanting to die, not wanting to live, jumping off the bridge, I felt that her suicide was a way for me to silently speed up my progress of success. And, with my near-death experiences, being ill and coughing for three months, and the longer recovery time of my body with each virus or bacterial infections (it took me three months to get rid of my previous infections), I thought what if my body couldn't combat these infections any longer and I must go. At any point now. There were several instances where my body didn't want to go any further with life. I had promised myself that I would not become one of those authors who would become famous after her death. That I would like my mother to enjoy my success, economically speaking, and I would like to indulge in my success too. But I don't think the publisher understood my intent because I could not, in my private, sad ways, explain to him why I was trying to flood the market. Also, sitting next to him, I kept on thinking about his urethra.

I also told him I might switch careers, meaning a career that would make fast cash. I thought about going into the movies. There was a part of my soul where I wanted to shut everything down. Like my mother, I would love to die too. That perhaps it was best I went first. During the conference, I had written Forrest Gander. People were flooding him with hugs at one of the panels. Cherimoya and I planned on going to his panel so I could give him a hug. But two security guards, the first one at the main gate and the second one at the panel's door, were blocking me from doing so. The badge cost $200 at the door and with me spending $10 a week on groceries for months and months, I couldn't afford Forrest's $200 hug. It cost me only 54 cents to purchase my flight there and back from LA. I stood outside of the gate, staring at the security guard and feeling helpless in all possible ways. I walked my mind through the different scenarios. I could flag a stranger down, ask him or her if I could borrow her badge. But who would, right? I thought about giving him or her my phone as a security deposit. All the shame I felt for being indigent and starving came flooding in. I thought about ignoring the security guard and just slyly sliding myself into the panel room. This state of desperation made me think of poor people who couldn't afford food and they had to rob grocery stores to feed themselves. I was just like those poor people. I was sure that in their despair they concoct ways in which they could steal or retrieve food. I thought about stealing people's badges. I could use the skills that I had learned from the TV shows *Leverage* and

White Collar, hours spent watching the duplicitous actors use their sleight of hands to pull an artful pilfer. Here, I could put my indirect education to good use. The more I thought about it, stealing wasn't worth it. Some poor poet might be stopped in the middle of entering a conference or book fair and have to be occluded from entering and then have to spend $50, which was a lot of money, to replace the badge. Except, I thought. Except. Except Forrest lost his wife and I may lose my mother and may be captured and put in an adult prison pen. I sat there, stupid and dumb and lost, waiting for time to pass through me. When asked if I enjoyed the conference and what panels I liked the most, I told them I wasn't there for the panels. I was there to hug Forrest Gander, but this I didn't tell them. But I couldn't even offer a hug. Cherimoya came out in the middle of the conference to sneak me in. In the book fair, she got me a paper bag–colored journal with matching pen, Valeria Luiselli's *The Story of My Teeth*, and a can of sparkling San Pellegrino. It was one of the first drinks we had in Providence. She still remembered. She told me about Forrest. How he was there, but wasn't there. How he was completely whole. No body parts missing. I sat there outside of the perimeter, my saliva drooling without me. I thought about the woman who sat next to me, another poet. Except she was white and she loved the works of Claudia Rankine and Roxane Gay. She told me that the conference yesterday was packed tight. Claudia Rankine spoke passionately about how racism was still prominent, that white straight dudes were still championed over the colored men and women. How straight white male authors were being given space, money, and resources for their work. That people of color were continually ignored. Here I was a walking example of this racism. North Domina hired a white straight dude from Princeton. I think life was trying to con me with irony. Or it was trying to spit in my face. I told Cherimoya to go back to the panel. I didn't want her to miss out. I sat myself near the cafeteria and thought long and hard at my badge-less self. Well, I still looked gorgeous. Even if my dress was three years old. Still not outdated. My mother brought this summer dress for me several summers ago when I was at still at Brown. The dress was a radiant dyed thing, slender and feminine. It looked delicious on me and still did. Most of my clothes were from centuries ago, but I didn't mind and no one had to know that it was old.

After I arrived home from the convention, Forrest

wrote me that he was busy and a mess and would love to meet any other time. I told him that my mother was suicidal and that we could be a mess together. I told him that I would be there for him if he would like me to.

The hardest part about the convention in LA was finding a place to stay. Cherimoya invited me to share a room with her peers at North Domina and I didn't feel right about it. Even if these were students I would not have, they were still students who experienced my interviewing process at North Domina. It didn't feel right and so it didn't feel right. I didn't book any hotel room ahead of time in part because I couldn't afford to. My bank account had gone down to the low two hundreds and any spending now would tip it over. I thought if I could recognize a friend or an acquaintance from afar, I could ask them if I could stay a night with them, paying them $50 or something. After attending a dynamic queer reading of a friend's partner and hugging Mr. Buddha, I walked up and down Hollywood Blvd near the intersection of Wilcox Ave in search of a motel. I found one. Motel 6, which cost $125. I begged the male clerk if he would lower it, but he refused to. He told me about the poor-quality motel next to it that I could use. I walked over. It seemed as if the "motel" came from a movie set. Not designed for real-life room accommodation. I wondered what you would think of me in this state of desperation. You had written on your blog about travel safety. I had read it months ago. The two male attendants who assisted me looked like two Mormon evangelists, dressed in egg-colored white buttoned-down shirts and black slacks, who had been kicked out of the Church of Jesus Christ of Latter-Day Saints and were forced to work in this squalid place in order to occupy a seat at the gate of Hell. They told me that they could only accept cash and that a towel cost $10 and if I wanted a room with bathroom, it would be another $14 dollars and I needed to come up with another ten for the deposit. If I returned the towel and the key, I would get $20 back. They told me to withdraw at least $78 if I wanted to stay for the night. I asked them I would like to see the room without the bathroom and the room with the bathroom. When he showed me the monk-like rooms with their wooden beds, I thought of a prison. I thought a prison had better living conditions. I smiled through the whole thing and asked them if this was a pretend place, not a real place, for a movie set or something. The Mormons told me: This was no joke. This place was as real as my skin and flesh. Desperate and not wanting to sleep on the street or at a twenty-four-hour diner, I told them I needed to go to an ATM. I walked all over Hollywood Blvd near Motel 6 in search for a CVS and a Western Union. I stopped by CVS to get one towel. I couldn't trust the insalubrious condition of the motel towel nor the bedsheets. Bedbugs were crawling in and out of my mind as I tried to shake them off while I went into Western Union to withdraw money. The ATM spat out receipts of error after error. Even though I had money in my bank account, I couldn't withdraw it. The bank wouldn't let me. This was one of the first ten signs from the universe that I shouldn't stay in that dungeon drug-selling motel. I stood there while a Black man and a Mexican woman stared at me, asking if I needed service from an Uber. Outside, a Black man asked me where I came from. When I replied, he kept on shouting at me about the Vietnam War. I was confused, but kept on walking. The men of the street continued to harass me until I entered a store where a clerk washing the tessellated floor with a mop told me that there was a hostel just a few blocks away. I left. I was still wheeling the beach towel with me that I purchased from CVS. They didn't carry regular towels and I thought it was better to use this than anything else that the motel had to offer me. It was so surreal to experience the upscale conference and then to wander aimlessly from one store to the next until I found the right kind of room accommodation within my budget. In front of the hostel, across from the LA LGBT Center on Schrader Blvd, I rang the intercom. The woman who spoke to me told me they had run out of room. I kept on calling them, asking them if they had a room for tomorrow. Eventually, a fat man came out telling me that they had a room for both nights for me and it would cost $101 with tax. I eventually went with it.

At home, my mother asked me to find her loan she made in September of last year and to give that information to her income tax man, Mr. Air Force One. She told me that breathing was hard for her and that she was tired and exhausted after her workout. She told me to do this for her. She told me that she didn't want to live and that she was exhausted with life. Earlier she had drawn me out of a nap to look for her Charles Schwab checkbooks she misplaced with her Fidelity checkbooks in order to pay this month and next month rent. I turned everything upside down in order to search it for her. I couldn't find it. I have been running around like a slave doing things for my mother so that her life would be easier and so she wouldn't commit suicide, but nothing I did seemed to help. It made it even worse. In order to guilt me into doing things for her, she would pull the suicide card. I knew this, but now there was an air of stiff silence between us, the silence had come after I berated her for not writing down the $80 she received for an alteration service. Later, when she would fill out her financial statements for six consecutive months, she wouldn't know what to put down because she wouldn't have had filled out the required data for it and she would want me to help her. My mother told me now that she wanted to retire. I asked how could you retire when you donated your entire retirement to Fidelity and Charles Schwab? She informed me her eyes were blurry and her eyesight had become poor.

Then, what saddened me most of all, was my mother's behavior toward me afterward. She called Mr. Air Force One to tell him that I didn't understand her condition and her sadness.

After my mother departed to sleep, an immense loneliness enveloped me. Like being beneath the sea. My entire consciousness dropped below sea level and all my thoughts were tangled up like seaweed. It was the sort of feeling that I never wanted to wake up to. At least my mother still spoke of retirement, but I was not sure if I wanted to retire. I thought deep down that I didn't believe that I ever wanted to live.

To push all my books out into the world and then die? A waste of life.

Even when the dishwasher came to life, I remembered where my body had been and that life was treating me like a poem. An erasure poem. Slowly, black strips covered where words about me should have been written. I was black and white and these blackouts were in the place where my memories should have been. My life had never been a piece of cake and I had been reduced to a juxtaposition.

By the time the dishwasher almost stopped crying, I had written you wishing you a great first day at your new job. You wished me a good morning. You told me that my message was so kind. You thanked me and you informed me that you just woke up to get ready. You wrote that you hoped I had had a wonderful time in LA. You blew three kisses in a form of consecutive X marks. You informed me that we would talk soon. I didn't know what we would talk about. Perhaps I could tell you about the time before my flight to Los Angeles, how my mother had sat by the lamp to sew the neckline of my black Bebe sweater made of 67 percent rayon or viscose. Through time and poor washing on my part, it was coming apart. The tag on the sweater said no "dry-cleaning" and no "machine wash." Or I could tell you how she had reorganized my luggage so that it was aesthetically compelling in a sense that everything was organized and stacked neatly.

Las
Vegas

I haven't written you since my arrival back to Las Vegas. I think about you intermittently like the way rain thinks about the earth. An intermittent desire. Pulling back a little, I haven't been engaging with you very much. I feared that with your new job, you would be exhausted or consumed by orientation and you wouldn't have time. But, you had time today. We spoke for a long time. And, it had filled me with excitement. An excitement I didn't want to end or depart from. Yesterday, I was trafficking Instagram and read something that made me think immediately of you. Poetryandwords had quoted it:

The best love is unexpected. You don't just pick someone and cross your fingers it'll work out. You meet them by fate and it's an instant connection, and the chemistry share is way above your head. You just talk and notice the way their lips curve when they smile or the colour of their eyes and all at once you know you're either lucky or screwed.

I didn't know why this made me think of you. But I did know. I did know that my love for you had arrived unexpectedly. And since I couldn't for most of our conversations see the colour of your eyes or your smile or if your lips curved or moved in a straight line, perhaps I could see arc and undulation in the lips of your words or the way you phrase a thought or the way you end a sentence. Maybe this was the colour of your eyes: the way you used sentences. I have grown more and more fond of you as time passes between us. I haven't yet decided what to do with this fondness. Leaving it alone seemed such an ache. Yet, to prolong it—the future might never arrive.

Let me revisit today with you. I was moved to share with you that I had won the Ronald Sukenick Innovative Fiction Contest. You replied that you couldn't wait to read it. To assure you that I had been waiting patiently for your letter I told you that I would go to the mailbox today to see if your letter had arrived. And, to excite me even further, you said that you had another one cooking for me. I'm having a hard time writing you letters lately because this manuscript feels like a gigantic letter to me. I'm not even sure if the mail carrier could even take it. I asked you how you were. You imparted that you were good and that you were sitting in your bedroom being quiet because your husband was massaging a lady in the living room. You asked how I was. I told you that I was happy. That makes the two of us, you said, and that you tried to copy my Facebook picture, the one I took at the LA Convention Center, when you were walking to your job on your first day of work. It was a quiet picture. Nothing spectacular, but I liked it. I loved your hair in it. It looked like it wanted to be angelic. The type that would only kiss the sun and nothing else. The manner in which you captured the photo made me to feel closer to the texture of your scarf fabric. You imparted that your hair was really long now. Plus, you only washed it every five days. It was your thing now. In reply, I rhetorically asked, "Didn't Napoleon tell his Josephine not to shower for weeks because he loved her fragrance?"

You asked back, probably not rhetorically, "Wasn't that from the poem 'Obsession' by David Citino?" You said you loved that poem. It was inspired by the news on NPR about a sixteen-year-old boy who, obsessed with smelling nice, died after months of repeatedly spraying his entire body with deodorant. You pasted the entire poem for me to read. I loved the last two stanzas.

> drying in July fields. And then
> you have the essence of love,
> good sense we sucked in
> at the breast. *I will come to you*
> *in two weeks,* Napoleon, knowing
> the sweet intensity of desire,
> wrote to his dear Josephine.
> *Promise me you will not bathe.*

This led me to tell you that my mother's nose was so sensitive. And you said that your mother's nose was too. You too had written a poem soon after hearing about the news of the boy on NPR and you read it to your workshop and someone said it was gross. Your mother always told you that you smelled like sweat. You confirmed that you did smell like sweat. I asked how you felt about it. You said you were angry and that you couldn't help it and that your mother could smell your breath when you walked through the door. And, quite expectedly, I told you about my mother's ability to smell. That she could smell the difference between Iowa and Nevada. You also declared like the way one could declare unusual items on a customs form for international travel that there were certain times when your smell got more sensitive, like right before a cold arrived, and you would feel like your mother. It wasn't difficult to share that my mother's sensitivity to smell drove me crazy. I imparted that my mother could smell all of my lovers. You replied by saying, "Holy shit." You asked what would I do or say. I didn't know how to respond to my mother. I learned that your mother could smell your desire and she'd slit her eyes. My mother, on the other hand, would say that my girlfriends had such a strong odor as if she expected me to change their odor. As if it were a sweater you could take on and off. This was where I learned you couldn't stop laughing. My gay friend could smell me when I was on my period. My period was filled with the smell of iron. You wanted to smell periods. You asked if I could and if my mother could. And we both could. I had a lover once and she loved period sex. You commented that you bet it was really hot. You wanted to try to smell. I suggested that when your friend was on her period to accidentally lower yourself and then inhale big and to let me know how it went. But you had something bigger in mind. Or, you said, you could just run to her and stick your head between her legs like a big crazy dog. You love it when dogs do that. You couldn't wait to try it. You were going to do it to your coworkers once you became friends. I replied that this was an excellent way to introduce yourself. This was the reason why you were getting a job. To be able to do this kind of thing.

It has been days since we last spoke. The last time we spoke, I nodded your way, telling you that I mailed you a letter. The last time we spoke, you were reminiscing with me about your previous one-night love with a man named Agostino. He was taken off an Italian menu I mentioned, from the menu of the best Italian restaurant in Henderson, which was just across the street from my mother's apartment complex. When I showed you the menu with scallops, you saw his name and you said that if you could order it off the menu, you would order him. The kind of love you had with him seemed rare. I walked away with this knowledge. And of your regret that this sort of love did not come often in one lifetime. You shared with me a picture of him. I noticed his baby-banana-shaped fingers. His teeth, I particularly liked. In the picture, you exuded a calm happiness, like a contented happiness, the kind of happiness that appeared to suspend from the ether of perpetuity. If your husband and you did not work out, you would reach out to him. The last time you interacted with him, you were acutely aware of his subliminal sadness, like a pair of wet duck feet padding in melancholy without the surface of water knowing its sadness. But how could it not feel that the duck feet were crying, even if they were already wet, and that the current was crying with them.

Whether it was with your husband, your past loves, or wherever you were in space with time and desire, I still felt connected to you somehow. I wonder if this connection will go away with time. For instance, when I woke up this morning, I thought of you. I thought I was alone in my message with reality. I thought it was an idea conceived from the nature of wishing time away. I also woke up with the thought and the non-vacant idea, like light into a home, that perhaps today was a good day to die. But today wasn't good and I don't know if tomorrow will be.

You wrote me to tell me that you haven't spoken to me in days. I learned that you had been overcome by the new job and now your mother-in-law was visiting and that you were using all of your patience to maintain. You informed me that you missed me. Your mother-in-law was grieving for her husband who died last year and it was hard for you to listen to. You had to relive your past with cancer, your dad and death, and grief for your mother. It was raw still for you. Your mother-in-law could be stupid and insensitive and also sweet, you said. Being with her made you miss your own mother acutely. You coped by meditating. You coped by walking forty minutes to the station to go to work. Here, I learned that you didn't trust your observations completely. Most of the time you felt people so clearly, meaning you understood what was going on underneath them. More than they did. Of course, you were sensitive to the subliminal. I knew this about you before knowing you. You noted that being sensitive, although tiring, was excellent for writing. I also learned that an Australian art magazine contacted you and asked you to write an article about young new gallerists in London. You thought it was stupid, but you said yes anyway.

I asked how your husband handled the domestic

turmoil. As if you were wearing the skirt of the cosmos and as if this skirt has spoken to me, you said that he was very patient and you believed he suffered and he worried about his mother. You could tell that he could feel your frustration and that he was torn. I imagined that you were a page inside of another page and that you were torn crisply clean from its definitive signature.

You asked what I had for lunch. I haven't had lunch yet. I was preparing bánh xèo. To help you understand, I said it was a Vietnamese crepe. I learned that you were looking at pictures of them online. You said they looked good. For dinner, you had halibut from the fishmonger. It was lightly pan-fried. You had it with steamed Swiss chard, roasted potatoes, and spiralized Mouli. I asked if you prepared all of this. It seemed so elaborate. Your mother-in-law and your husband cooked. You must have watched them like a hawk over two dancing mice wearing similar flippers. And so your day went along. You said some new baskets made of hay arrived at the studio yesterday and they had a powerful animal smell and you had to move them to the other side of the room and all of this arrangement must have made you think of me. I suppose I was now associated with odor. Our last conversation was about odor.

My former roommate, Cherimoya, has flown to Missouri. She texted me, "This place is TINY. The airport is an airfield. An empty field. The airplane's maximum capacity was 5 people. I was swamped by white people. I just landed." My platonic tenderness for her had grown out of proportions. I felt a deep sense of protectiveness toward her. She was petite and Muslim and I feared that people would mistreat her. She texted me, "The smallness of this town has descended on me like a bag of bricks." I kept on telling her to become a lawyer. The life of a writer belonged to economic impoverishment. My mother kept on telling me to tell her to pursue law.

Before this, you noted that you always gain weight when you went to your mother-in-law's. You also got constipated due to dehydration and nerves. I had to impart that the last time I was constipated was 2007. 2007 was a good year for you. You started going to therapy, you stopped puking, and you fell in love with Antonello. You had puked because you couldn't digest your sadness. You had lots of panic attacks. Lots of bad things happened at once and you still hadn't gotten over your dad's death. I told you that I was glad you were no longer in the puking phase. What you revealed to me seemed comical to me.

You said that the last time you saw Antonello, you got constipated. You didn't eliminate for twelve days. I didn't even
know that was possible. After you saw Antonello, you flew
back to London, took a dump, and never saw him again.
As for me, I didn't generally experience constipation. Even
before 2007. 2007 was the diarrhea year. My body rejected
all kinds of food. Food my body could take before.

The following day, you had spoken to Finch. You were
nervous. I had published you. I wanted to publish her, but
because our friendship was no longer, I couldn't make the
prefect chess move. You had been nervous about telling
her. You asked about my mother. My mother was a mess.
She has lost her ability to function as a human being. I
went crazy this morning, helping her prepare the ques-
tionnaire for her bankruptcy lawyer. Helping her take
an online course about bankruptcy. She couldn't see the
numbers. She has lost a quarter of a million in gambling
debt from day-trading. Her credit card debt and loan grew
to $90K. She couldn't make her nearly $4,000 monthly
credit card payments. Her phone rang nonstop. Clueless
about bankruptcy and disapproving of my mother's money
management skills, I sat there near her, feeling pent-up anger. I had told my mother that this was unfair. To place the

burden and weight of her error on me. Yet, it registered no guilt or sorrow in my mother. She blew it off as if it were nonsense. I wanted her friend to relieve the burden for me. She called her friend, the one who worked for a collection agency. Oh, the irony. To help her with her bankruptcy. He came for two seconds and he escaped into the ether. I was left alone to deal with my stress-inducing mother, who would cease to function like a normal human being when it came to her debt, but could sew shirts and pants for customers like Clotho, Lachesis, and Atropos all at once. My mother became these three goddesses who presided over the needle and thread of fashion.

Perhaps the cosmos felt sorry for me. A friend in Vegas had flown to Tennessee. She read my delicious baby book and wrote to me that my writing was highly emotional and physical at the same time. That it evoked emotional and physical responses. Primal was a word she would use to describe my work. She observed that my writing wished to be experienced. And that as long as the reader was open to the experience, liking or not liking the work was secondary. She noted that I was an immersive writer and the wonder of my writing was that one never knew if I were being revealing or playing with the reader. Then, she wrote,

"If you had been with me when I read your book, I would have asked to kiss you. I hope that does not upset you. As I said, you were immersive." Well, that was that.

My mother's memory continued to disappear from her. Tonight, as she sewed and altered a dark dress for a client, she couldn't find her presser foot to do her transparent sewing. She turned her entire workstation upside down in order to look for it. Her client was going to yell at her so I got on my feet and helped her search for it. If I were a presser foot, I would walk away from the sewing machine too. Especially a machine that made me run fifty miles per hour. I discovered the foot hidden in a light orange bag inside another translucent bag.

Sleep deprivation left me in the cusp of nothing. I couldn't think and write. I was struggling to sleep. I kept on thinking about women who had been raped. I kept on wondering if rape was a gender issue or a power issue. I was trying to understand so that I could voice this concern in my new novel. You were taking a bus home when you wrote me. You were nearly home. For some reason, in my mind, your front door was red. Though I wouldn't know and I didn't want to ask in case it shattered the fragile impression I had of your door. The situation between your mother-in-law and you had improved. When you arrived home, you told me that my letter had arrived.

I was making spring rolls for dinner and I asked my mother if she wanted some. When my mother lived alone, her diet consisted of anti-Vietnamese cuisine. The repulsive redolent condition of fish sauce drove her insane. Like sầu riêng (durian), she couldn't stand the odor, but loved the taste. Tonight, she devoured fish sauce and said that the spring roll was an exciting dish to eat. Caucasian cuisines such as salad did not seem to embody pungency.

These cuisines appealed to my redolent-inducing mother the most for their lack of smell. But I think she turned to salad to annihilate her past existence. She wanted to evacuate her Vietnamese from her overzealous assimilated American self. I think for her, reminiscing Vietnam was a return to a lack of civilization. In my cooking, I tried to reinvite my mother to embrace Vietnamese dishes more, asking her to not abandon the place where we had been born. I believe the reason why I loved fish sauce was because it embodied the sea for me. Specifically, the Pacific Ocean, where I spent three days and three nights inside the sarcophagal body of the boat. We were trying to escape Vietnam, my family of six, with other families too. There were thirty of us in a tiny boat. The fish sauce seemed to coat and distill the salt water of the ocean. Going down on a woman reminded me of eating fish sauce. I often thought of my lesbian body and the lesbian body of others and the diaspora of taste. There was comfort and security in being with a woman as it brought me back to the concealed vessel of my childhood. Sometimes I wonder if I was born as a lesbian in order to escape Vietnam or if when my family escaped Vietnam, I became a lesbian or if the ocean or nước mắm (fish sauce) turned me into a lesbian.

My clitoris has stopped having a conversation with my desire. It reclined dormant in my body like a cat. For days, it had meowed nonstopped. After my LA trip, my body discovered the abyss in its abbess. I had found its silence annoying.

I have missed you, lightly, and at times, a great deal. I vacillated between the two binary worlds. I missed you because we haven't spoken since the day you received my letter and you showed your mother-in-law your zucchini flower thought. I haven't been contacting you. In part, I didn't know how you would respond to my letter to you. I had drawn you, a cartoonish sketch of you in the kitchen making fresh pasta from scratch with your husband. I had drawn you because I wanted to celebrate and convince you that your friends were silly to deride you for cooking for your husband and this was a beautiful thing to capture and should last like ink on the drawing page. A part of me wished to withdraw from engaging with you. There was no moral code for this. Your husband is your husband and my desire is my desire. But then, with your nuptial existence, I wanted to keep my distance. Another part of me wanted to explore and differentiate the difference between desire and the collapse of desire.

My mother as you already know hasn't been feeling well. She vacillated between wellness and unwellness. One day, she was a thunderstorm. The next, she was a tattered tree, broken in a windless wind. My mother's depression, I believe, though I am no medical expert, has somaticized into physical symptoms such as a reoccurring fever and headaches. Though when I googled about reoccurring fever, it informed me about blood cancer and other rheumatic and indigestible things, obscure things. And infections. But, mostly, I think my mother is ill in the head. "If you alter your perspective," I tell my mother, "you will alter the condition of your disease, from having all kinds of cancerous manifestation to having none." I believe in this. I believe the mind is capable of controlling everything.

In the world, there were many earthquakes with many deaths. One in Japan and one in Ecuador. The Ecuadorian state had more deaths. I thought of you in London, maybe isolated, maybe not. Suicide bombs go off everywhere. You could easily lose your limb and I mine at any given moment. As I read the news this morning, a happy paraplegic using a *Blade Runner* limp had a smile on her face as she ran. She ran that marathon to conquer the inner Boston Marathon bombing massacre in 2013. She was a former dancer, you know. Do we use our legs to dance? Or do we use something else? Or will terrorism and war make us all eventually bionic? As a collective human race, through the auxiliary callings of bombs and explosions, are we dispersing our flesh like debris now? Will this be the ultimate force that moves us? To get rid of the corporeal prison that prevents us from accessing other concealed, atomic corridors of reality?

I spent last night reading an article in the *Boston Review* by Ed Pavlic, who has taught my book, *The Vanishing Point of Desire*, in his class about the racial tension in America. He narrated his own personal view, growing up with racism on the back and forefront of his consciousness, on his body and on his intellectual body—about race not being the color of skin. I used to think that America is making progress—the civil rights movement and the continual efforts. But to be quite frank with you and to break the sad news to you, the world hasn't made any progress. In fact, the fact that we think we have made progress only makes us retrogress. Affluent white males' plantations shift now to prison clothes, prison meals, prison walls, prison barbwires, prison shoes, prison food trays, prison everything. And the obscenely affluent white males and white police officers and authority figures are enjoying their wealth through prison bids, concrete and all, smoking their gigantic cigars while drinking premium whiskeys. Racism today has moved toward translation, not transformation. The law must be broken down. Prison walls must be broken down. We change our historical clothes all the time. We do this frequently and rapidly to give the world the illusion that we have a body and a soul. We are truly soulless.

My mother's customer, a pimp, walked with a cautious hunch and avoided the police. The white world he lives in doesn't appreciate his existence.

He has taught my mother how to steal money back

from sweet-lipped men who stole money from her and blew her off. He has given my mother advice on marrying rich men. He has told her to set her pecuniary conditions high. "Hannah," he tells my mother, "you must ask these men for a down payment of two hundred K, if they were serious about dating or marrying you." I thought of my mother as a real estate property, having acres and acres of land. I thought of my mother as an expensive plot of land on which a businessman would want to build his condo. Though my mother has dated millionaires, she found their presence and wealth cold. One millionaire, who owned a hospital here, had his house in a gated entrance, not even a gated community, but a gated entrance solely for himself. "Whenever I drove up to his castle," my mother narrated, "it felt like I was going to prison. His castle was cold and icy and womanless. It isn't even a home." "It's not important that you marry a rich man," I tell my mother. "If he is kind and thoughtful, his thoughtfulness and his kindness is your wealth. But if he has lots of money and he is an asshole, then marrying him only improverishes you because he cannot and will not share his wealth with you. In fact, marrying him will only make you poorer. This was not a good way to spend the rest of your retirement."

It has been six days since we last corresponded. You probably thought that I didn't measure the distance between us and I let you think so without correcting you. A simple word or two of asking how you are would have broken this distance. But I measured this distance every day and with frequency. Coupling this thinking, I have been also been thinking lately about suicide. I have been trying to convince my mother out of it, but I wonder if I should. After all, I don't think there is much in life worth living for. I used to think it was love or the way leaves twirling in a sea of asphalt that made life worth staying longer, but as I sat in an incandescent ennui with my mother's back to me while she sews, I think if I die in the immediate present, I wouldn't be able to hear Mạnh Quỳnh's music pulsating through my heart or the riveting sound of my mother's sewing machine breaking my heart each second of my expired breath. And, in an equal response to the binary code, if I die right now and right away, I wouldn't have mattered just as the breeze of several days ago wouldn't have mattered to the trees, which got to experience its tantalizing passing. We wouldn't want to desire to go on because we were occasionally tantalizing.

Cherimoya called me not long ago. In fact, in the

midst of me rewatching *The Shawshank Redemption* for the hundredth time. She had phoned to tell me that she had been craving chocolate the night before. My gift of books and chocolate made it in time to fulfill her cravings. Your gift should be arriving soon. She phoned to tell me that brilliant people with great talent often did not win awards. We learned lately it was whom we knew that dictated the size and dimension of our accolades. I told her she must learn how to beat the system: meaning she must learn to adapt. An abrupt, awkward conversation ensued between us and I ended up departing from the conversation to let her be.

In this empty space between us, should I ask you now, "How are you?"

After a week of hurried living and an enormous distance between us, the umbilical cord of desire and need between us has been severed. I feel utterly disconnected from your life in London, though not completely disconnected from you. I saw the skyline photo of your London, the one you captured, foggily, and my heart throbbed. It throbbed because the city was utterly beautiful and you were residing in it without me. It was the omission of my existence there, I believed, which made it even more beautiful than ever. It reminded me of Li-Young Lee's poetry collection with an intimate, relatable title, *The City in Which I Love You*. I almost wrote that to you in an Instagram response to your photo, but I pulled back, fearing that the reply may suggest that our friendship wasn't entirely platonic on several levels, the emotional level in particular, though my carnal desire for you has died a little bit each day and now my body felt utter silence for yours.

I learned soon after that my package and the journal in which we accepted your work had arrived to your door. You informed me that the mailman had to ring the door for it since he hardly ever rang the bell and that your heart was swelling with happiness upon its arrival. I discovered rather quickly that you had a difficult week. Your brother-in-law, after seventeen years with his company, was fired from his job, and his wife, your sister, dealt with her stress through the stomach. You had to say goodbye to your mother-in-law. I wondered if it was a good thing or a bad thing. Each time I won a writing contest, I become terribly skeptical of its presence—that it was capable of making me dead inside and I wouldn't have any will to move. I feared it may change me from a person who desired transformation and change to a person who desired stagnation. I fear success can lead to all forms of paralysis, especially the emotional and sexual ones. Being a stone is easy. You just stand there like a stone and even a butterfly may occasionally wish to visit you, even sit on you, or cling onto you like a cliff-hanger, or even a pigeon may even want to urinate or defecate on you, but if you experience emotional paralysis, you would see everything passing through you as if you were a throat of a sink pipe and water just washed through you. You would stand outside of yourself, watching yourself lead a vacant, dismantled, liquidated existence. Not even a pigeon would be moved to exercise its small asshole on you.

Your boss, whom you haven't met, had written you numerous emails about the balance between work and life and then she had asked you to stay longer at work. It was an exceptional week and normally she didn't ask you to stay longer than you needed to.

My mother had become less suicidal as if an angel had opened a door inside of her and she was exuding light. She was working through herself by watching Vietnamese news on YouTube. She frequently talked about Minh Beo, who had been incarcerated for his sexual exploits toward youth. I devoted afternoons to teaching her new English words such as the words: "irony," "obsolete," "innovation." My mother was a famished learner and devoured my teaching like a child who discovered water for the very first time. Learning, my mother, told me had made her head clearer and she could think better. My job was to increase her brain cells so that she did not resort to suicide as a life option or an alternative. I am still very much a student of life.

As for me, I found myself frequently restless and tired. My poetry collection was coming out into the world and officially on Amazon the third day of May. My work, which was published by a very small publishing house in New York, did not have the strength of advertisement like the bigger presses and my mind had to work hard to figure out how to disseminate my work to more places and people. I vacillated between hope and hopelessness.

Nadal won back-to-back clay tournaments, one in Monte Carlo and the other in Barcelona and his success made me enormously happy. I had been rooting for him not so secretly and after his loss in Australia this early January, my eagerness for his success went on a walk toward despondency. With his injuries, it was hard to know if he would ever return. At forty-nine years old each, Rafael Nadal and Guillermo Vilas shared the same number of titles. Of course, I want Nadal to also win Roland-Garros.

I kept on thinking that I needed to write a bestseller as if I hadn't written one. And as I stepped back into myself, to consider where I was in life, I realized that perhaps I had already written a bestseller and it was waiting for my permission to spread its achievement widely and it was on its way for its opulent triumph. Which of these books—soon to be launched—shall cast its net the widest?

We think the riches are far and away from our reach, but what if your poverty came because you were too blind to see your already emerged wealth?

I shifted this thinking today. Today I own what I do not own. And tasted what I have already tasted.

The day I left Sin City and stopped combatting my mother's suicidal thoughts and cheering her up from her bankruptcy doom, I was taking photo shoots of my mother in various dresses along the outskirts of the desert—where we saw miles of rocks and soil and dessert blooms while the entire strip and its skyline were ahead of us. Later, my mother's friend described the photos of my mother in the desert as perennial things. My mother being the flower that bloomed out of the desert. Because my mother's photo shoot was a success and because the photos came out arrestingly, my mother forgot her appointment with the bankruptcy lawyer. We rushed quickly as my mother quickly undressed and changed her fancy dresses to pedestrian clothing in her beat-up Lexus, only worth about five grand now. And we rushed quickly to the lawyer, eleven minutes late. It was also the day my mother signed the paper in the office of the bankruptcy lawyer. My mother's debt to all creditors totaled $114,293.00. We learned that my mother's debt was pale in comparison to a woman who gambled away her own mother's $1.6 million in investment money in real estate. After her father passed away, her mother found herself wealthy in large acquisitions of money. The mother still doesn't know. One man owed debts to 140 creditors. I didn't even know that was possible.

The Venezuelans already lost sleep in order to save electricity. Signs of "No hay luz" blanketed the Venezuelan stores. And what about their health care crisis? I have already flown into Chicago. I got into the train heading into the city, I snaked and snuck into the city like an eel. My morning was half spent at the Chicago airport in search of plugs. The train into the city had already shut down. When floods of airport workers entered the baggage carousels, I thought of their lonely bodies in their sleep-deprivation clothes. I thought of their 4 a.m. sacrifices as they worked hard to raise their children. To bring food on the table. I thought of the decades of my mother's sacrifice to raise us to be adults in the States when she had nothing on her back.

It's not that I haven't been thinking of you. But you are now sleeping in the back of my subconsciousness and although I could wake you, I choose not to wake you. Love is dangerous to a species that has gone back to bed.

The last time I entered Chicago, you were writing me, telling me that you had written me a letter and you needed an address to mail me. I was waiting in the security line, waiting to be xrayed, waiting to raise both of my arms up. I have stopped wearing bras with supporting wires to avoid being frisked. My breasts did not lift as high as they did before. They circled around in their lowly world getting entangled in the grease of movement and in the brass subjugation of my bumping knees. And when I returned, your silence indicated that you had moved on with your life and I am still jobless, seeking a destination in my state of homelessness.

The naked landscape of the train left me in a state of fringe and marginality. I felt I was on the border between

life and death, with the conductors intermittently inter-
rupting my naps with announcements of arrivals and de-
partures. The blurred landscapes took over and my eyes fell
back into their circles of absence and ennui.

The
Midwest

When Cherimoya called me Fatty at the train station, I knew she was happy to see me. I rushed into the bathroom to evacuate. The sandwich I had at Subway did not get along with my stomach. Cherimoya tossed my luggage in the short-term parking lot and waited for me in the airport lounge, not too far from the prayer room.

In the evening a day later, I made chè thưng and offered it to our neighbor. I debated. I undebated whether to give it to her or not, but in the end, I decided that after my roommate, Cherimoya, convinced me that not saying "hello" would be rude. The neighbor welcomed me back and was excited to see me. I was happy to hear that at work, they hired a boss, a female boss, and things were going to change. Fingers crossed.

It has been nearly two weeks since we last conversed. Time flew over me like a lost kite. I didn't know it was that long until I opened my calendar to measure the days and the nights between us and two weeks seemed like a deck of cards of memories, which I took out to check the switch-blade of their speed before putting them back into my pocket. The last time we spoke, it was obvious that I would not have an address for you to send your missive. And, now, the address was before me—yet I felt weak in giving it to you. I have missed speaking to you—not for any definite reasons related to eroticism—I missed the ardor of getting to know you—of your words on the screen, of what you had for breakfast in that monstrous city, that London of yours. The weakness arrived not by enervation, but because I did not know if I could bear the pleasure of getting to know you again. Your new job had occupied a large and raw aspect of your existence—yet I could feel the fiber of our nearness—across that big lake that separated me from wanting you. The days had been so long—Cherimoya and I drove to Iowa City to do my reading at Prairie Lights in her small vulnerable Chevrolet that would hiss violently if it went over sixty-five miles per hour. She and I were crawling through the bleak tunnel of the highway—the eyelids of the headlight blinked brightly. I must let you know that I am quite fond of Cherimoya—her presence ever so intelligent and ever so sharp, yet the mundane tasks of cleaning and cooking were creating an inevitable distance between she and I. She hardly did any chores—after long hours of cooking, I must wash everything and then washed everything after we ate. The work was laborious for one person—I felt dead inside after I cooked—rushing to tackle many tasks. And, I felt lonely. Doing everything by myself. She would hover over my shoulders—asking insincerely if she could help me—but I knew deep inside she didn't mean it and it hurt. She would on purpose perform things poorly so she could get out of it.

We had guests over tonight. Her friends from class came. We served them sangria and tacos. Tacos were Cherimoya's favorite dish to eat. I was exhausted from getting everything ready. Since we didn't have a table, I spent some time sweeping the floor, in case our guests decided that they wanted to eat there. And of course, Cherimoya hadn't cleaned the bathroom since I left two and half months ago. I thought it was considerate to have a clean bathroom for our guests. It was intentionally making the place hygienic. Tacos were finger food after all. Cherimoya was hovering over my shoulders, asking why I was cleaning. She followed me around while I cleaned, demanding to know why I was cleaning. It was exhausting. Yesterday was exhausting as well. I made Cherimoya a dish because she came to me hungry, wanting food and she didn't want to cook it herself. I started tossing things together—rice noodle this—sautéing vegetables that. She asked how she could help. I asked her to stir the pan for me because it was difficult to chop the cabbage and stir the red onion at the same time over medium-high heat and I wanted her to babysit it. She kept on asking me why she must stir. I kept on asking her to stir it so it wouldn't burn while I chopped. I despised Cherimoya in the kitchen. I ended up multitasking and did the dish all by myself. I felt bitter afterward and couldn't stand to be in her presence. I should stop cooking for myself and for her. I didn't know if I had the courage in me.

Having only slept one hour before the reading, the drive to Iowa City felt like being on an operating table. The surgical blade of light. The smell of the car exhaust. When I leaned onto the podium to read, I felt like the night had bathed itself in amnesia. When I stood on the podium to read at Prairie Lights, I felt myself moving backward into the ether of air as if I had drifted from one ammoniacal to another ammoniacal sphere, drifting away from the readers. The reading went poorly in my eyes. I knew the words on the page and the words that came out of my mouth made sense as I read the words from left to right, but my existence alone did not make sense. I could see the readers from the peripheral angle of my eyes. I could see them like their faces were T-shirts and jeans being blown back into the vacant fabric of air. I thought of you so very briefly in time. You had suggested the idea of me reading in London. I have missed our conversations. They seemed light-years from now. Even before the time of the dinosaurs. Perhaps now, your existence arrived to me like clusters of light before dispersing.

I knew there was an audience from the internet listening in—I knew of their existence, but when I stood on the podium, I forgot they were there, a radio-length away from the extension of my mouth.

I spent all day vacillating between life and death, between suicide and moving forward, between eating a peach or a plum, between peeling my eyelids off the wall or the floor, between stroking the keyboards or the legs of the table, between submitting myself to vacancy or ennui, between climbing the bed or the bathroom stall, between putting on my eyeglasses or upsetting my perception of reality, between the rape of Samburu women or the My Lai women, between cutting myself with a knife or with a scythe, between taking my hands off the keyboards or my eyes off the door, between being dead or being unreasonable, between sleeping on a mat or on an inflatable mattress, between texting or smelling the water pipe, between shutting off the fan or turning away from the ceiling, between the spoon or the fork, between inserting myself with a carrot or a dildo, between reaching out or reaching forward for the cashews, between the swollen purse or the canning table, between hardships or belonging, between solitude or loneliness, between ending or starting a new life, between working hard to be even more poor or to be already poor but working less, between the cup or the rim of the glass, between embracing the easel or losing the paint.

A surprise birthday celebration compelled me back to Iowa City once again. I had planned so poorly. I did not even book a car or a bus ticket. I have been thinking of you intermittently, like rain. The falling of the thought, the thought of you, on the shoulder of my mind. I think of you like the way dust thinks of vacuum cleaners. When it's near the presence of the vacuum cleaners, the dust becomes scared. My days became shorter as I languished between Facebook and facing the future. There were book tours I must book—yet, not yet—my mind suspended itself in the air of time—like underwear on a clothesline.

I had been thinking of you intermittently like rain again. The thought became small and smaller like becoming a grain of rice. It was not too late to give you my current mailing address. I had asked you to wait and you had been waiting and I had been wanting very much to disclose my mailing address to you, but fear got in the way. The closer we become with our correspondences, the higher the risk becomes. You were married after all. In your latest Facebook post, you revisited your wedding album with your Alzheimer mother and your Italian husband. The images were bright and green and lush like you had walked right into the Eden of heaven. Seeing the images and seeing myself looping out of your reality, I had halted my desire for you. It was sitting on an immaterial seat of limbo. But then, I remember, you said the passion between you and your husband had come to a halt.

Meanwhile, when I woke up, I realized that unfairness shares a dual life with success. If one knew how to harness it properly, like converting a negative energy to a positive one. My roommate Cherimoya talked about her negative experiences with a performance class she took where two professors co-instructed a classroom badly. The power dynamics shifted heavily toward the masculine professor and the students suffered greatly. The female professor failed to defend her students. The professors arbitrarily assigned the grades. Unfairness like this was important for the students on their road to success. Before the accumulative effect of unfairness, the students' writing now has unfairness as a wall or as an unlikely opponent to bounce their writing against, and thus, would grow tremendously as a result. One needed an echo to gauge how strong one's voice had become. Unfairness was an effective measuring device for this and should be used frequently obscenely. Without this opponent, unfairness, the students would simply drift into a writing blah. Students who wrote well or tried to achieve writing well or who wish to succeed greatly will face more unfairness than another because their standard had become higher. The angst that reclined beneath this ardor of unfairness was a sign that Cherimoya would write better than she had before. And, in this sense, I was excited that unfairness came to her and it also came to me—for her in the form of the classroom and for me in my job interview.

After watching the documentary film of Ai Weiwei, I turned to Cherimoya to tell her my inner thoughts. I dreamt one day everyone in this world will hold each other's hand and then walk together into a gas chamber. Later, when I walked over to the typewriter, I noticed that Cherimoya had recorded my voice: collective suicide. Prevents innovation.

I haven't had the desire to wake up in the morning and nothing had the will to excite me. If the nature of my soul on this earth floats on the sea surface of existence as a cork, then life, the submarine, is submerging me, weighing me down. Each morning and each moment of my existence, I am that cork that circles beneath the bottom of the submarine trying to find again my buoyance for life. Each day is an attack on this vision of release. And I don't know if you feel this way about life, but if God were kind and if, near now, toward now, I am not at the door of success, meaning that each day I am not searching for a way to economically live, I ask that God puts me to sleep forever. And, when I die in my sleep, as it is a gift taken away from God, I ask that he also invites my mother to die in her sleep as well. She has suffered enough already. If I do find my buoyancy again, will it mean that I will roast forever? On the shifting bed of the sea by the burning radiance of the sun? While drifting perpetually into nothingness? If my existence were that cork that corks someone else's mouth, like the mouth of a wine bottle, would it mean that I inevitably find myself, randomly, sitting on a stage, that dining or kitchen table, waiting to be impaled for a celebration or the death of a celebration? I want to love life, it seems like a benevolent thing to do, to love something that doesn't love you back. I want to write you to tell you these things, but lately you are in your London flat or home, loving poetry more than ever. You and one Daisy and the rest of the nightlife of London.

To make matters worst, Cherimoya noticed an art exhibition nearby. She thought it was the coolest thing to do on a Friday night. We went. But there was an entrance fee of $5 per head. We went to two ATMs, the first one didn't work. When we entered there were many white people gathered around a darkly lit demonstration of pottery making. A woman molding a vessel in front of us while some dancers pushed each other around like grapes being tossed inside of a broken salad spinner. There was the tossing of light and a food truck inside the barn-shaped space. We ordered sushi and chili soup—the worst Cherimoya ever had. Everything was a waste of money. There was no monetary discount for the worst exhibition that I have ever seen. We dragged our excited souls back home— where Cherimoya took a nap and I oblivioned into watching YouTube videos of Russell Peters making fun of his Indian parents, of different kinds of Asian people on the planet, of his asshole being forced outward to kiss cloth on a military airplane, etc. I also saw other comedians like Joe Wong and his immigrant narrative on rowing and wading, the one with the PhD in Molecular Biology. And the Iranian comedian Maz Jobrani on hijacking strawberries when sending greetings on an airplane. Which made me miss having a friend named Jack.

Yet, what have I attempted to do, dear life, but find the will to live? What have I been doing to curb this overwhelming sadness? I checked out a stack of books, beautiful books from the art of ballpoint to culinary books, but nothing seemed to ignite a passion for life. I have also watched five to ten minutes of Bruce Venture porn—his bicolored dick made me think of a fried sausage that wasn't dipped properly in a deep fryer. The tip part never made it in. There was rawness to it. His dick was long like a long train ride. The kind of train you want to get off—but you can't because you can't seem to find its exit point. Some of the women were in a reclining state, their neck in a Swiss army pose, his butt and back to their head while his bicolored apparatus entered their mouth. It mesmerized me each time—the woman's lack of gag reflex and the discomfort and pain they must endure to stage such a seemingly elegant mechanism. His body and the way he performed the standing sexual position made me think of a water bottle manufacturing plant. The machine lifted, lowered, and then capped the bottle before it shot the water bottle out onto the conveyor belt. If sex has turned into an assembly line, has the human body shifted from being a nurturer to a manufacturer? What kind of sex industrial revolution is this that leaves the human soul barren, alienated, subjected to perpetual impotence? A few days ago, at a chicken manufacturing plant, workers were de-granted from bathroom breaks. The company was cutting down on the number and duration of bathroom breaks a worker could "abuse" as if one could abuse nature emergency calling. Some chicken plant workers began wearing diapers to prevent accidental urination and defecation. I think of babies in diapers cutting chicken thighs into bite-size pieces. I think of the juxtaposition of odor: feces and raw chicken wings. The result? An amputation of the nose and modernity.

To prevent my mother from engaging in any more codependent behaviors toward me I told my mother that I believed in her. She texted me in the early morning asking me how to say something to the furniture guys at RC Willey. The gift for Mother's Day from me was a free delivery service of her purchased furniture. My mother was unhappy with the size of her sofa—she said it was like an elephant in the room and she wanted to return it. She kept on calling for small tasks and the requests kept on weighing a toll on me. My mother does not know how hard she makes life for others. She lives in this vacuum space. And I think psychologically, one wishes that one lives in the world where our loved ones care so much that instead of making the lives of the people we care for easier, we make it harder. No human is moved to be kind. Marina Abramović, yes, the grandmother of performance art, gave people permission to do whatever they liked to her—regardless of her well-being or safety—they willingly ripped her clothes off, scarred her with a knife, spit on her. What had she done but provide them with this permission to do anything to her? Why did the audience choose to violate her? My own mother doesn't choose to hurt me, but in my devoted desire to help my mother, she knows that she could ask unreasonable things and I would do them, unwillingly, screaming, terrified in my state of unwillingness. She kept on asking me to help her file her bankruptcy papers, and knowing nothing about bankruptcy, other than the knowledge that Donald Trump was well rehearsed in it, I helped her again, against my own desire. I kept on thinking that if my mother loved me she wouldn't ask me to do this. This forced task. Yet, based on that condition, my mother had no love for me. She kept on asking and asking. Task after task. Relentlessly adding more of them. I would be in this state of utter terror, worrying about my own thing, worrying about how I am going to put my books right into this world and she would climb on my shoulders, begging me to do things for her.

Sometimes I would gaze at my mother with utter hatred, thinking, ah, this is how mothers love their children. After saying no to her, guilt the size of a massive cloud would consume my existence. I kept on thinking, "What if she dies, and the one thing she asked me to do, I wouldn't do?" The question wasn't how could I live with myself, but how soon I could die afterward? How soon after my mother's death could I die?

By now, you probably want to know what is happening in the world. Nadal lost to Djokovich in the Italian Open in Rome. I love Nadal, I must say, very much, but Djokovich's mental game has won me over. He is currently the man with belief. And those with an utter, monstrous belief invited to themselves only enormous success. When two players share a similar and comparable skill set, if one player wins, it simply comes down to pure mental work: who has a more superior belief system than the other.

Other things also happen in this world. Lightning strikes eliminated fifty people in Bangladesh. A North Carolina man was charged with a federal misdemeanor on a Southwest flight. He yanked the hijab off a woman's head and shouted, "This is America." Religious rape of this nature isn't like a missile crisis, but each unwarranted attack on a Muslim should be treated at an atomic level: with every fiber of our being, like a missile crisis. If we truly cared, we wouldn't force-feed them with our bigotry. We would be elegant and ask them to randomly inject the Maz Jobrani strawberry, Tourette-style.

In the afternoon, when Cherimoya went on an OkCupid date with an unknown male she had accidentally encountered at the grocery store (I asked her, "How did you know it was him who messaged you?" She replied that he had a distinct face.), I wrote more pages for my new nonfiction book and read the news about the flogging of Saudi blogger Raif Badawi, husband of Ensaf Haidar, who was sentenced ten years in penitentiary and one thousand lashes for "insulting Islam through electronic channels." And, I thought about when should I read her book, *Raif Badawi, The Voice of Freedom: My Husband, Our Story*.

I have been sleeping on the floor, on a white mat folded over itself. The mat is shorter than me by a foot so when I sleep, my feet lopsidedly touch the floor. At times, the sudden jerk or realization of the uneven surface wakes me up in the middle of the night. Sleeping like this, I think about my poverty a lot. And, how at thirty-six years old, I was like this, homeless, lover-less, and in a constant state of utter terror of where I was going to sleep or eat next. My unemployment benefit is slowly dwindling. I would only be able to last three more months or less. It seems like this tortured state is ever so endless. The thing is, most of it I could cover up, like dressing well in my old beautiful clothes. We haven't spoken in nearly a month. But once in a while, I see a post from you in London, and it's nice to know that you still exist in this world.

The thing with scarcity for me is that after my graduation, the last three years of life have flogged me over and over and over again with the lashes of poverty. Over one thousand of them. More than one lash each day. Some days when I win a writing prize, it feels as if the flogging has halted for a bit, but soon, it returns with an empowering force that is closer to debilitation than death.

Each day I try to imagine being in a relationship with a woman or a man and each day my imagination turns its back on my desire to imagine. For so long it has not been possible for my body to fall asleep concupiscently, I cannot ask it to wake up. I have been walking around the apartment, trying to jump-start my desire after the battery of it died out. Each day is a fight against ennui. A fight against a dormant condition in the mind. Against mental paralysis. The barrenness of emotional fields. Yesterday Cherimoya went on a date. She had some desire left, but mine went out like a blackout in New York. I gazed at her with sadness. I wish I was as excited to go on a date like her. I tried to imagine anyone I could fantasize. No one wanted to be a part of my fantasy. I could even invite my imaginary lovers to come to my noetic party. I have become so pathetic and sad, really. My mind has found emotional and sexual love to be repulsive. In fact, the blackout for desire is so great that masturbation has become a social chore.

Each day I imagined cuddling with a woman and when cuddling with a woman didn't work out, I imagined cuddling with a man. And soon, my entire existence began to shut down. And, each time it shut down, I felt so tired and burnt out. Not like a candle near the end of its wax, but like a pot of broth without any broth left and the burner kept on burning. And my mind was sitting on the floor of the kitchen, scraping the burnt off. I had been in this state for months, even years. I found love so repulsive that I wondered if I would ever recover and be normal like everyone else, sexual creatures of this earth still living sexual and emotional desire. I wondered how long I was going to be this way. The thought of dying alone didn't seem to make me flinch. What made me flinch was the return of feeling nothing. A little dead inside that seemed a lot.

I tried to fix myself by being myself, allowing me to be me, but there is something very fucked up about this. I kept on thinking of my mentor, C. D. Wright, and how when she was still alive, I had desire to keep on going, pursuing things, advancing my place in the publishing world. I thought of the time when I had arrived in Providence. I don't remember how I arrived there, but C. D. Wright said she would meet me. Without asking if I needed my luggage carried, she impressively advanced toward my wheeled suitcase, wheeled it to her Toyota hybrid, and lifted the entire luggage with ten of my books and clothes into the trunk. She turned to me, "I am scrawny like a tree, but strong and sturdy." I believed every word of it. She knew I couldn't lift and had been lifting a lot during my travel and wanted to lighten the load for me. When I entered her car, the tears I held in nearly spilled out of me like beans and they were in the midst of running away from me. I knew this even when she hugged me and told me that she loved me.

Or that one time . . .

After three weeks devoid of interaction, you wrote me.

You wrote, "It's been so long since we last spoke it's like we've been swallowed onto the tongues of clams. How are you? Are you still traveling? I'm almost finished with deadlines and after next week life will be fresh water again and then more poems will come. I hope you're having sensational thoughts wherever you are." I replied that indeed we have been clammy. I told that you that I haven't forgotten the class and I told you that I didn't know how to manage everyone's schedules and that people were falling off the class like flies. I told you that I had only taught at a university level and students would just show up and I taught. You told me that I was not God and that made me feel better and that management was impossible. Later you told me that your friend Ruth, an endearing name for me, would give you a cigarette if you asked and that you said you smoked once in a blue moon, but you didn't look good doing it. I told you that most people don't actually look good doing it either, especially their insides. You thought some people looked sexy smoking, but then they smelled afterward. I did date a woman who was a smoker. You asked if her pee smelled. I didn't know what to say. My intimate interactions with her were strange. But the guy who kissed me was almost a smoker. But he smelled great. I never saw him pee. Immediately you imparted that your first boyfriend smelled like egg salad. And that the last smoker you dated was in 2006 and he was also an alcoholic. Soon you would be meeting Maggie Nelson at a reading. Also, Eileen Myles was coming to town. You said that last night's reading with Chris Kraus was nice. People were laughing and I assumed giggling and they were friendly. Last year, you went to three of her readings and it was tense. With an art school crowd and academics, people were competitive and your cheeks got hot. Last night, you asked her the same question you asked last year, but she didn't really answer it again. You had dinner with her a few times last year, but you were so diffident. In a few weeks, you were going to do a reading at John Milton's house. You wanted to wear a robin's egg blue dress with your cleavage. In which case, to go with your dress, I should recommend the rectangular-cut Oppenheimer Blue diamond just auctioned at the Four Seasons Hotel des Bergues at nearly $60 million, $57.5 million to be most accurate. The late Sir Philip Oppenheimer had showered his wife with this exquisite stone. He must have been slightly fond of his wife. The key word here is slight. Oh, Blue Moon of Josephine, you lost. Not too badly, but still you lost to something nearly flawless.

I had halted my desire for you and it had worked. I had trained myself to stop wanting you. And it had worked. The human mind can make the human heart small like a burglarized Bulgari diamond and when in doubt, smaller than a ruby Serpenti bracelet.

We ended up talking about Milton. I told you that Milton compared himself with the Virgin Mary and that he viewed his grandiose poetry as a child. How his poetry was like a child, Jesus. How it was like his second coming through his poetry.

Lately, in my waking state and semi-soporific state, I began to theorize why I've omitted myself from engaging in a romantic relationship with anyone. Is it physiological? Physical? Purely psychological? Is it the problem with plumbing? Mechanical?

I thought and thought. With a heart condition, the quality of making love and making out decreased drastically. In order to make love to a woman, I needed to be on an oxygen tank. Oftentimes, I would get out of breath, my body lacked the proper blood circulation. My hands would turn blue and purple and it took me days and even weeks to recover from a minor exercise in fucking. Nowadays, if it were a major exercise, I would probably face death before she reached orgasm. I would have to teach myself how to breathe again. Giving women head was psychically painful for me. I couldn't please women very long and when I did, I would be so oxygen deprived. Perhaps this was one of the reasons why my desire for Cherimoya ended so quickly. I would go down on her and she had a beautiful body as if her upper organs were designed for fucking and lower body meant for swimming. But for whatever reason, our love session would end rather quickly because I could not stay down long. It was like diving—a human body could only hold its breath for so long. Cherimoya would complain that I only wanted to be pleased—at one point—she called me an asshole for lopsidedly providing her pleasure. I had naively thought that if I couldn't please her as fully as I desired by not going down as long as I could, at least she could enjoy the pleasure of my body. But it was her pent-up angst held so long, like the way I held my breath for her while making love, that exploded in the death of our desire. After she called me an asshole, I shut down completely. For not equally reciprocating her in the art of cunnilingus. While I couldn't dive down into the small aquarium of her body, I had found other ways to please her, but by then, it seemed her sexual aesthetics had changed. She no longer desired to be whipped. Ultimately, I shut my body down and when I did, I stopped having feelings for her, and soon, it was inevitably obvious that the romantic nature of our relationship also ended. Our preexisting friendship resulted in her conflicting loyalty to our former tryst and prevented her from seeking out other people, though I encouraged her frequently to date other people. Most likely, the men and women she would encounter would not share the same medical fate as I had and she could properly enjoy sex fully with another partner. I had begun to accept this as my new terms of letting go and of moving forward with the relationship.

After her date with the male philosopher, she came home complaining about her stomach. It was the pleasure of pain she was complaining about. She told me that they made out for a very long time, to the point where her stomach ached. She had not exercised this muscle in a very long time. And, I understood this was my limitation. I also understood that my desire for her had died a very long time ago or perhaps I never had the desire to begin with. She told me about her making out session with a guy for the

first time. I suspected based on the way she semi-clothed
the degree of her pleasurable experience that the encounter was a success. I began to question how long it would
last. It was her youth and caprice to share this new pleasure with me as it could only isolate her from me. When
she told me that they made out without losing breath, I
thought of my own limitation. Mainly, it made me return
to the inevitable. The word "odor" revisited me uncondi-
tionally. Besides my extremely low oxygen tank, I couldn't
embrace the intensity of her odor. I had to stop breathing,
in the already breathless condition, in order to please her.
I couldn't take the intensity of her odor. When I stopped
breathing, the time I could spend on her clitoris decreased
drastically as well. To combat this odor dilemma, I encouraged her to wash her genitals with soap, but a trauma
in her childhood prevented her from shampooing. When
she was small, her sister had used soap to wash her genitals
and the effect of the detergent stung her and left a scar on
her where she would be terrified of soap onward. On top
of this time reduction and fear of soap, I couldn't invite her
to let go. When I entered her, it had to be at a precise angle,
at a precise time, and how and where to place my finger.
Lovemaking was an organic process—there was nothing

organic in our lovemaking—it had to be artificially manu-
factured and controlled to the perimeter of centimeters.
The way she wanted to control the content of the bedroom
and the content of our desire made it unconsolably un-
pleasurable. The eloquent power of fucking relies heavily
on the release. Slowly, her directed guide toward how to
make love to her became an impossible chore in which my
performance would end up not pleasing her at all. I shut
my body from her. And, I began to enforce the platonic
platform. She would try to make sexual moves toward me
intermittently. I would neutralize it by making ineloquent
kung fu moves. Sometimes when I wasn't fast enough or
when I didn't know how or where it was coming from, she
would pinch one of my nipples and I would yelp violently
like a dog that had been kicked. I began to gaze at her with
disdain and I thought to myself, one day she would realize that, despite my medical limitation, I had been a lovely
lover to her and that I had treated with kindness. She
wouldn't realize this until much much later. When years
have passed and she would have exchanged handshakes
and intimate places with many lovers.

After her pre-fucking encounter with the philosopher,
who, she informed me condescendingly gazed down at

her intelligence, Cherimoya continued to persistently call me "babe" or "honey" or what endearing terms she could concoct in the moment. Because Cherimoya appeared petite and almost childlike, her intelligence wasn't perceived or taken seriously by the academic community. But Cherimoya was very smart and those that underestimated her smartness would be doomed to know much later the effect of her intelligence. I had asked her numerous times to stop calling me in these terms, but she kept on advertently making the mistake, which was no mistake. She blatantly disregarded my plea. This was her subconscious calculated tactic to control me. She had voiced this control when I told her I wanted to hang out with her friends and my only friend. She told me, "Your time here until I leave for New York should be given to me only and when I am gone, then you can get to know them." She laughed it off as a joke, but having known Cherimoya intimately for three fucking years, I knew this was no joke. I knew that my finance was limited and Cherimoya wanted to exploit this economic weakness of mine. Cherimoya was going to subsidize my sublease of her apartment. In exchange, I would keep myself from socializing with anyone. In exchange, I would cook and wash the dishes and she wouldn't lay a single hand in the distribution of chores. I knew she didn't love me. This was no way to love someone or anybody. I put up with it anyway. On top of this urge to control me, she also didn't tell her landlord about her residency. She would hide me if someone came to the door. It could be anyone innocuous as the UPS man or a woman begging for food. Under the pretense of fear, she would say that it was the landlord Kelly making her rounds, visiting or checking on us. On the lease, she was the only tenant. And, if the handyman came by, she would tell me to hide in the closet or in a room until he finished with the fixing because he might gossip about my presence with the landlord. I put up with all of this. Yet, anything I applied and Cherimoya helped me apply, to economically advance myself out of this cycle of poverty, only fell flat. The Hodder Fellowship, for instance, supposedly for emerging writers, was a joke. A slap in the face. Only people who had accolades and accolades and who had a solid footing in the publishing world could even have a slim chance of being considered a candidate for it. You wondered how someone as tiny as Cherimoya could have a hold on me. It wasn't Cherimoya—she was merely a conduit for it—who had such a strong whipping grip on me. It was an ogre named poverty. The same ogre that the supercat Puss in Boots was trying to swash out. The one with the monopoly on wealth.

Sometimes, sitting side by side while we were reading together, I would look at her with compassion and at other times with contempt. Under the secured thought that she was benevolent by subsidizing my sublease, she thought she was a great person who was generous and kind with me. In some ways, this was true. She had been more kind to me than other people. But her kindness came with a condescending prize. The same condescending gaze my sisters gave me when they knew I had no place to go and sneered at me. The people who we think loved us the most ended up loving us very poorly. It was merely their grandiose logic that blindsided them and made them think that their benevolence made them impervious to criticism or ridicule.

I held this all in me, like a festered scar that wouldn't go away. I kept my mouth shut, yet kept my distance. I somewhat tolerated their obscene behaviors while at the same time convincing myself foolishly that it wouldn't last forever, but it had lasted for years. Especially during the time when I was in a domestic abuse and my psychological state was whipped to a pulp. We let abuse go on within ourselves for too long, not knowing when the cycle of abuse, neglect, and poverty would end. Humans, by design, are machines made to torture other humans and living things. Under the false Darwinist theory that we are designed to survive. The truth is simply: We are here to exist and then to torture. Either to inflict torture ourselves because we convince ourselves that we are God's messengers and we give ourselves the authority to sanction punishment or we torture others and even ourselves because we think this is the only way to have an ontological sway on God, meaning that the only way we feel we validly exist is to turn torture into a physical and psychological drill and use this drill to make an ontological dent on existence. But is it possible that God validates his own existence by inviting enemies of God to nail holes into his own son, which is himself, which is merely another corporeal dimension of God? Without this drill, we are unmarked. Immortality doesn't forgive us.

Even when Cherimoya controlled me and did not love me, I thought all of it seemed meaningless. Given the kind of relationships I had been entering, it made sense why I chose to stay abstinent. There were no reasons for me to love or be loved. God is God and I am woman. And, if

God were a woman like me, he wouldn't design torture to look like an apple tree. Some idiot would say a pear tree instead. And some say he would design torture to look like God, but I would design torture to look like wind chimes.

If I had a choice, instead of escorting pairs of animals to enter the ark, I would defy God by inviting all the animals for a wind party, in which I would pierce the ears of all animals such as an impala or an elephant or an owl and I would put fancy earrings on them. When they walk or sway, the wind would make them chime. I would intend all earthly creatures to become wind chimes and when they would walk into their death, that flood, while beneath in the biggest, instantaneous aquarium ever built, the propelling force of water would pull at their earlobes and turn all metal into seahorses with segmented equine armor and while these monogamous seahorses would hydrodynamically spiral in and out of seagrasses, we would begin to accept that earrings would replace the species of human just like we had replaced dinosaurs with us. If earrings were the next pseudo–*Homo sapiens*, we would see that reproduction wasn't designed for survival, but for the sake of beauty.

I am all for wind chimes.

In the days ahead, I am preparing my exit. There has been a lot of electricity in the air, fiber and glass, clinking their incandescent bracelets of banality. Cherimoya's family did arrive—they arrived in the middle of late spring—layered by traffic noises, the frequency of ambient air. They arrived and the apartment, without proper ventilation, smelled like a marijuana manufacturing plant. They smoked a lot of pot, languishing from one afternoon to the next. I felt dizzy and eventually a pounding headache came to meet my head. I reclined in the dark hours too, thinking of my pot-less self. In this state, even the mountains would grow long horns. But I loved their Muslim presence, they vocalized themselves from one vulgar state to the next, tossing profane words left and right and in tenderly disturbed ways, it was beautiful. They fought with their bodies and tongues. Throwing themselves around with a loving force. When they fought each other over minor things for the pure joy of kicking each other around, they smiled and flirted with each other's wounds mercifully outside while blowing soot from the chimney of their lungs. Perhaps I envied them a little. For the way they loved each other just enough. Sometimes, when I leaned back into the green chair, I thought, was it possible to fight this way? And, still love each other dearly, dearly as in enough? I thought of the wounds in me that could never self-mend themselves. I thought of my former self, drinking a glass of tears each day. Spilling the salt. On the tilapia. Could we suffocate anyone with the depth of our sadness? They stayed for four days. Though they did book it for seven days. Cherimoya, in her intolerable impatience for their visit, moved the seven days to four. I wanted them to stay longer—to inhale their differences.

My desire for Cherimoya's sister remained quiet like a plum. I didn't act on the chemistry—though if I wanted the betrayal to arrive fast like a train before derailing, I would have shamelessly leaned in and kissed her sister's lips to savor the taste. When she came to visit in the late fall of last year, my cunt throbbed nonstop and uncontrollably. I had craved her sister's feminine soul like an animal and I kept it there to myself, telling no one. Not even a spider as it crawled slowly by. But on the day of her visit, I couldn't help but tell you about this latent desire. I wrote you and you responded. You told me that since my attraction toward women appeared so infrequently, perhaps it was wise to act on it. I had told you that I joked with Cherimoya, asking her how would she feel if I dated her sister. Naturally, Cherimoya said she wouldn't be very happy and would not like it at all. She stated this so simply. So matter of factly. It would be a betrayal indeed.

My voice remained voiceless.

My taste buds remained morbid and moral-less.

The following week I began to date a police officer. He had a fetish for his motorcycle. Every day, my typewriter sat in the corner and sobbed. No one listened.

In the end, I decided to end my friendship with Cherimoya. Her love for me had changed drastically in the last six months. She grew a new personality or perhaps the antidepressant alprazolam she had been taking made her too gregarious, too outgoing, too sparkling for my taste. Her thoughtful essence changed. When she interacted with people, words fell out of her mouth like a bitter betrayal. In order to blend in with the white world, she hung out with white folks. She dated a white man and shared things I had confided in her. But I am ending it for more psychological reasons. I didn't like the person I was becoming in her presence. I perseverated frequently and I was obsessed with my own dilemma, my own financial crisis. My impoverished state of mind. Her new world was a golden snow globe. I felt cold being in it.

When I left it, the snow was still falling.

And, most disappointing of all, Rafael Nadal, after winning matches in the first and second round and achieving his 200, had withdrawn himself from the French Open due to a wrist injury. This news took me by surprise. I had been in the Nadal cave for too long. For other matches, he had injected his wrists with horse tranquilizer to numb them. It has to be either horse tranquilizer or nothing then. Some parts of the tennis world are heartbroken. Without Nadal stopping him, Djokovich would have his opportunity for his first French Open.

The French Open continued to be riddled with rain. The red clay soaked itself into a state of lacquered delirium. I have stopped caring so much about it. Except for Serena Williams. I wanted her to beat history. When I think of her playing tennis, I think of her galloping away on that black horse of hers. All the other horses behind her, so far from her, at a great distance. I prayed that she would never have to use horse tranquilizer to tame her horsepower.

I thought by abandoning you for a month, I would be okay. I thought if I kept my distance, I could reinstate our bond. I thought if I were cautious, I would have you as a friend. I have fallen for you again. It came unexpectedly—I have come to learn that love could not be controlled. I could not hold it by the mane and ride it. It came to me yesterday while I unconsciously and blithefully wrote you. I asked you how you were. It was so tame and nonchalant. What came after it left me craving you on and off, intermittently like rain. Not the rain from America, but the rain from Paris. The rain that came with the French Open. The kind of rain that made you withdraw your umbrella too late.

You told me that you read my new poetry book at the dentist this morning while they did a deep cleaning. You wrote me that you have many things to say about it. You have been saving your thoughts. To inflame my curiosity, you wrote, "I LOVE THE BOOK SO MUCH for many reasons." I was surprised to hear that you had read it since the book would not be opened for purchase and delivery until June 19. You said you ordered the book from the United States. I suspected that you couldn't wait for it. Reviews raving for the book had been coming in intermittently like rain. It made me so happy. You wrote that you couldn't wait to tell me how you felt about the book as you needed time to collect your thoughts. But first you wished to tell me that it was so intimate to read my poems in a collection. After having so many conversations with me, you said, it's so good. Every line surprises you, you said. You asked me how I was. Besides the fact there were over seven hundred migrants drowned in three Mediterranean sinkings, in the inside, I was radiating with bliss. But before I was happy, I was sad. I told you that I was sad and you wanted to know why. I told you that I went on a date with a man. For the first time in seven years. That he was very chivalrous. He took me on his motorcycle. We dined on a lake. Floating like an ether. But I felt so sad afterward. It has been about month, but this was your first weekend feeling calm. I told you that a man could be so sweet and romantic and I did not want him. You were going to watch the Champions League final tonight. You wrote last week about it as an English lesson. To curb my sadness, you told me that your friend David from New York called you this morning to tell you about his date last night. It was a first date with a woman he met online and she showed up drunk. She told him she went to an Ivy League school and he said "That's amazing" and she didn't like his tone so she slapped him. You laughed hard for one minute. You have felt that sadness before. You have felt it lots of times in lots of dates. You wanted love and connection so bad and being treated kindly by someone and it not being enough and the other person not being the one you wanted. You asked me what made me feel so sad exactly. I told you that I felt great sexual attraction for a man. Like I wanted to be fucked. But I also felt emotionally disconnected from a man. It was like having a nice pot. With the wrong lid. Both items are beautiful in their separate ontological entities. You suggested that perhaps I didn't want to throw the pot away. You asked who's the lid. I said that the emotions were the lid. I have told you this before, but I have not fallen in love with a man before. There is always this barrier. The separation between a body and its emotions. While I told you this, you told me that you are picturing me throwing the lid and my emotions sail through the air like a Frisbee and someone on the other side of the lake catches it. I thought this would be beautiful. When you said this I thought of you. You who lived across the lake. Later I learned that you used to have this terrible anguish over sex. That it would ignite these emotions and then they would have nowhere to go and the man would just disappear. And, now when you do it, you said, I assumed here you meant sex, nothing ignites. I asked you what happened? You said you didn't know. You said you didn't give a shit. You said it means nothing. You said you'd rather not do it. I had been feeling the same way with everyone in this world, but with you—I am bound by this infinite passion for you. Even when I tried to abandon it, tried to interrupt it, it came back with a force greater than its original desire. During the time of sexual currency, I often thought about leaning on a tree and falling asleep. I told you I feel a lot of sexual urges for a tree. In my blissful state of awareness, I wrote that it sounded kind of odd now that I typed this declaration out. You laughed. I imparted that I thought intimacy was hard to find. Much harder than falling in love. You agreed. Intimacy generated the best sex, I wrote. The best intimate sex you had turned out to be one-sided though, you wrote. I thought it was your lover with the thumb. But you de-confused me. I had been confusing all of your lovers. Your Italian lovers and your defecation habits. There was one lover that made you constipated. I couldn't remember which. But it was the boat lover that you never had sex with, but had incredible intimacy.

The more we talked the more I wanted you. You wrote, "Today I went downstairs to the farmers market beneath my building to get some vegetables and someone said my name and it was this Russian girl that I went to Oxford with years ago. She didn't like me back then. But she was happy to see me and know that we live in the same neighbourhood." I asked why she didn't like you. You replied, "I was loud and exuberant and not very serious or competitive. I've liked her all these years. I loved how she took herself so seriously. It made me laugh. She wasn't unkind to me. Just indifferent. I have another interesting story that gives me tingles. I will save it for your letter so I can tell it properly." I disclosed to you that I would be without an address for months. But I asked that you save it for me. At the rate I am traveling, I don't know when I will have your handwriting again. You were worried. You asked me, "How will you rest your weary heart?" You also asked Chris Kraus last week why she and all her characters moved all the time in her stories. Why she didn't describe interiors? And, it annoyed her. You were not sure why it annoyed her. It was your perception. Like a little needle. She didn't answer your question. You had asked her the same question last year and she didn't really answer. She was also deaf or was greatly hearing-impaired. I told you that perhaps being deaf might be a good reason why she didn't respond to your question properly. You asked if you could send your letter to a friend's house before I got there. I also told you my sadness was largely due to desiring

Cherimoya's sister during her visit and having to ignore that desire and stuff that desire into the deepest compartment of my existence. We talked briefly about your wedding and wedding performance and your desire to expose your boobs during the ceremony and about the hot photographer who made you uncomfortable and then you asked if I got married, where would it be. I wanted my wedding to be small and private and in an orchard. Pastoral. Rural. Desolate. In some of your wedding photos, your nipples were visible. While I have very little interest in exposing my nipples, I celebrated the visibility of yours.

Throughout the day, I thought of you frequently. Often in intimate terms. We were dining together at a remote, suburban place: my body on your body. I thought about making love to you just about everywhere. My lips buried in your neck. Everywhere, your skin. The tone of my ache. The resilient nature of our hunger. I thought about the atmosphere of your tongue. The density of our lovemaking. The first time my fingers would run through your body. These fugacious, fragrant thoughts as they covered the entire continent of my imagination. Mainly, I wanted to understand the geometry of our intimacy. What if between us was not a lake? And if our nipples when integrated were not mountains? Then what? If my hips and your hips were not two sedimentary rocks collided by time. And if my muscles were not the river that pulled your thighs into my river? What then? If we do ever make love and you reciprocate the content of my appetite, I imagine our lovemaking would be gentle and vehemently ardent. I imagine that you would measure how long it would take your kiss to arrive to the doorstep of my body. That you knew what I wanted before I knew what I wanted. That when you touched me— that touch had already trafficked my skin decades ahead of its human time. I imagine that our fucking would be interlaced with the different ribbons of emotional and intellectual discourses. When I kissed the back of your neck, it would be a place where a heartbeat opens its first provisional door before pulsating into a fit of radium. But more than anything, I wanted to understand your body like I have never understood a body in its short lifetime. I wanted to understand if our caress has brevity. That if you came to open yourself to me would passion have a limit. If the pulsation of pleasure would become schizophrenic or filled with an untamable madness and that madness could be only remedied with more tender fucking. I also wanted our coital union to be animal-like: primal, unreserved, neurotic, absolute, unstable, fervid, and electric. I wanted to know you in this way. In a vigorous, fanatical fashion designed for the human, not ethereal, element. I wanted you in more ways than you have ever imagined.

If the time spent knowing each other is foreplay—would meeting you be, in its full form, concupiscent bliss? Most people fuck because they have to fuck—but I think I wanted to fuck you because there was no other way to be. Our desire would have climbed these high stairs. At the top where there would be no more steps—we would fuck as if through fucking we named an intimate evolutional human event like the first time art was carved into the wall of the cave or the archaeological discovery of the Venus of Willendorf. I wanted to know you—to know you is to obliterate you. To fuck you is to fuck the statuette of time. To find that nonhuman center designed for the priapic collision between two untrained humans. I wanted my caress to peel away a layer or add another layer to your ontological cosmetics. To fuck you is to seek for the other elements of touch. We wanted to be that umbrella that asks the rain to reverse its vertical momentum, to retreat back into the sky—because the earth like the skin needs to learn to rebuild its absorption configuration for that caress that isn't ever just a caress.

In the middle of the afternoon, I opened the screen door into the banal, subdued Midwestern town. My face was an aluminum can of tears and I stepped out, leaking my body behind while the body in front of me, which was my only body, moved forward into the natural air and sunlight, the post-breeze of Chicago. I was crying, feeling utterly alone in my bed of human weeds, the kind I had been too lazy to mow down, the ones I left to grow wild in the garden of my spirit. My upstairs neighbor, like me, was in between screen doors too. Her body half-leaking like mine, except she didn't look like a villatic overture of tall grass. Her deceased husband was an artist and had died of cancer. When she showed me his paintings, I knew I wanted it for the cover of my poetry. The timing of it was perfect: I was seeking a cover and her husband's painting was available for print. In response to his death, amongst a million other things, she restarted smoking three weeks after his departure. Nearly a few human shadows from me, she looked neutral and dormant and as human as possible. Not wanting to submit myself to the ardor of loneliness, in that lightless space of apartment 616, I ushered my body forward in hopes of catching a glimpse of her fading form, hoping to make contact with another being, to divide my loneliness into small proportions so that others could bite into them too. She unfaded by stepping from the darkness into light and greeted me and not before long, tears spilled out of me like a bag of navy beans. She sat me down by the green bench near her smoking spot. The air was twirling with the late afternoon light. I told her in three days I would be leaving this place permanently. That my love for Cherimoya was one-sided. That she was too young or rather I was too young and she was younger and although there had been no romance between us, I had indulged her like a sexless wife. Someone I had informally returned home to—like family, she was someone I would cook for and with whom I satiated in the long, vacant hours of daily living. Yet, Cherimoya, post-romance, treated me obscurely, dividedly amongst her friends like a peony. She left me in the sunless corner, forever forgetting to water me every other day. I grew lonely and sad and unloved. And neglected. I had not been able to keep my delirium to myself and perhaps she had gotten tired of me sitting like a pot, absorbing my dark sunlight and not wanting to absorb.

The neighbor sat next to me, absorbing my sadness. She

understood that I had been taken for granted. Without disclosing the entire content of my melancholy, she sat next to me and understood. She understood what could not be said. I didn't need to tell her that I had waited hours and hours for Cherimoya to come home to be my friend. That I had tried to be friends with her cohorts, with her peers from the writing program in order to alleviate the burden of being with me twenty-four hours of the day— yet, fearing that her peers and friends would like me more or enjoy my company more immensely, she told me that I could not hang out with them until she departed for New York. And, the one friend I was socializing with—the one she wasn't close to, the one who made a move on everyone in the program, the one the whole program hated with contempt, was the one whom I felt hanging out with would be betraying her and her peers. So out of blind loy- alty, I sat at home and watched the strategic response unit soap opera *Flashpoint* for hours and hours and it seemed months would bleed into years. It made my sobbing worse, and worse than sobbing was that I wanted to be a police officer afterward. An emotional sniper who could alleviate anyone of their own pain of existence. I could not destroy the illusion of my loneliness, I had been living morbidly besides it. But the neighbor understood as she had been alone too. No one has put me in solitary confinement other than poverty itself, but I could have been a delirious item of some sort like a laughing walrus, crying out from my snout, confusing silence for gregariousness. These horse-whales were gregarious marine mammals, were they not? And I was quiet like a door, was I not?

New England

In my last stage of loneliness, I stopped desiring you. I stopped wanting you. My eroticism for you ceased to exist. As if the moon had stopped showing up for cosmic work. Moonless my world had become. I tried to fantasize you when I entered Boston from Chicago, but it felt forced and so I left my imagination alone. I stopped nagging it. I stopped asking it to be erotic. In my grief for obliterating Cherimoya from my life, I found that there was no point to yearn, to crave, to seek. Everywhere I went,

I saw my friendship with Cherimoya dispersing like seeds. Like a maniac, in my own mind, I began to squat in that memory Woor of mine and began to collect each seed that fell from the sky of my grief, my memory of our 3.5 years of friendship. But the rain that came raining down on Rhode Island and Massachusetts also rained down on my memory floor and flooded my vision of the seeds. I texted you when I took the wrong bus after the train arrival at the petite, remote train station in Kingston. It rained monstrously. The sky seeking revenge on trees, stop signs, silhouettes of light, and on women carrying large bags of groceries on Route 4. The windshield wipers wiped rainwater from the faces of glass and the wiping screeched like hyenas while talking to itself. I got off the next stop, stood alone in the bus canopy box, and leaned against glass. My silhouette had become someone else's light. I didn't expect the pluvial world to be ballads of beauty, but to lean onto something without someone or the mountain holding you, anyone could break apart. I was breaking apart like clumps of rain from the sky, breaking apart before hitting asphalt.

After seeing my tears fall like rosary beads, my neighbor offered to take me to Chicago. I had planned to read during the two-hour train ride to Chicago Midway. But, I wanted the company of my compassionate neighbor. I wanted to know more about her grief. Why she decided not to remarry after her husband's death a decade ago. In her minivan, she told me about an experience working with Joan Mitchell at an exhibition in California or France. In a dire need to release her bowel of urine during an exhibition, she asked the director if he could point the way. He said he would take her there. It was an understatement to say that he misunderstood her. Hard of hearing, he led her to a sculpture of a man. Duchamp would have been pleased. Already-made bathrooms were the new fad. It was hard to say where we were in the conversation. I had been making her a long list of books I highly recommended, more specifically for her. I recommended J. A. Baker's *The Peregrine* and *catku: poems* because she had a cat and the cat was fat and Mary Gaitskill's *Veronica* because I thought she might find great delight in Gaitskill's derision of psychological-sexual realism aligned with the culture of terrorized love. More to the point, she had been working with Joan Mitchell, who treated everyone dismissively with flicks of her fingers. I asked my neighbor why she was this way or why did she treat everyone she encountered like cockroaches. "You know I think she was ignored early in her art career and she was fragile and took this personally and she never forgave them for neglecting her," the neighbor contemplated. The neighbor had also worked with Jorie Graham's mother and Jorie Graham herself on a printmaking/poet project and asked me if I knew Jorie Graham personally. I told her no. But I was fully aware of the flood in Iowa City that submerged and deluged her entire shelves of books stored in her basement. When I think of Jorie Graham I think of her drowned, swampy book collection. Long gone. Floating away from her. Years of accumulation and autographed memories in a water-ridden sarcophagus. For C. D. Wright, she lost everything in a fire.

The train that was supposed to take me to Kingston left me somewhat abandoned. I took Bus 66 toward Kingston, but I was going in the wrong direction and waited at a bus stop at URI, University of Rhode Island, to retake Bus 66 heading in the opposite direction. The one-hour wait time made me somewhat anxious about missing my appointment with the photographer. I asked the bus driver if he could drop me off at Wickford

Junction, which would shorten the cab ride by about twenty minutes and that those twenty minutes would save me from the expensive cab fare into the villatic Kingston. When I arrived at the station that Sunday evening, the doors were closed and the railroad station was vacant. My heart dropped ten kilometers to the basement of my toes. The rain threw a long tantrum, long downpours that bled the earth away and everything was sky and rain delirium. I thought perhaps this was a good time to plug my broken S3 Samsung into its outdoor jack where the rain was clothing its socket and execute myself so I wouldn't have to deal with the photo shoot appointment or the rain. I tried to call a cab, but no cabs existed. I got desperate and even called a limousine company from Saunderstown, Rhode Island, to see if they could come and pick me up. The lady driver said that if she weren't already booked, she would come for me.

I lurched and tottered me and my dreary self and my luggage of four items (camera bag, computer bag, book bag, and suitcase of clothes) out into the sky that had ceased crying like a spoilt child and dashed for a place that looked remotely like a church or a funeral home. Midway through crossing the street, the spoilt child burst out crying again. This time hiccupping and burping, I was sprayed with liquid dust once again. A tan car turned into the station before pulling out and slowly hummed its way toward my footpath. An elderly lady, retired perhaps, rolled down her window and asked if they could give me a ride. I gleefully took the offer. The man who drove plugged the photographer's address, after asking for it, into his dashboard. His sister, a psychologist, sat behind him, in the back passenger seat, and her lack of hearing or her lack of auditory memory or her lack of attention compelled her to mishear everything that came out of my mouth and the brother and sister in their seventies bickered back and forth joyfully like husband and wife. Except the driver's wife sat in front. Her lips sealed like a licked envelope. Her presence sealed with a stamp and by asking her about her education background, I learned that I could be a letter opener if I wanted to. Both the driver and his wife were English majors and she had just finished reading *Light in August* and I took this time to tell them about my books. The sister took out her notebook and wrote the title of my book down. She mentioned briefly that she wasn't too keen on the technological age and that she was still dabbling in pen and paper.

The kind driver took me to the door of the photographer's home and chivalrously carried most of my luggage to the door. I didn't know if I should hug him or squeeze him. He was kind like an apple tree. If I had been impulsively compelled, without constraint, to hug him, I would have shaken him until there were no more leaves or apples on him.

I entered the cabin of Kingston for the photo shoot on self-belief. A coiled tunnel of white fabric was clipped with giant clippers to the wooden ledges of the balcony where the loft resided and were floating down to the floor. There was an immaculate orifice that led to the entrance of the vertical tunnel where the subject could enter or exit. The set was designed for the entrance of one subject only. At the end of the shoot, the photographer and I and another subject sat around the coffee table to dine. The photographer had prepared grilled corn, grilled beef patties, grilled potatoes, grilled asparagus, and grilled mushrooms. He was serving pinkish wine and the topic of the conversation was about dream flow. It must be the new movement, something outside of the sphere of my awareness, but others were fairly acquainted with the crusade. The subject spoke to me about a gay man who would enter her mind-space without asking her permission because he had acquired such an ability through training. I asked her, "How is that possible? To self-invite oneself into someone's consciousness?" But this gay, male yogi could. I was skeptical of this dream flow. This ability to be invasive or mentally allowing someone to hold another hostage. I told them about my skepticism. I depicted events in this lifetime like a deck of cards. More like humans were a deck of cards. They get shuffled around and if a 6 of Clover sat next to a King of Clover—there was no significant meaning other than the meaning that they were designed to sit side by side on that deck and if a 10 of Hearts shared an intimate vicinity with a Jack of Hearts—their temporary co-residency did not imply that they were destined to marry, to build a house of desire together, or even be remotely connected in some significant way. Sometimes sharing throbbing walls with another was just merely that: throbbing walls. But people put too much meaning or significance into things and space and intent and pure chance. This overkill of overthinking of overanalyzing of over-connecting could violate the existence of self and others and one's sense of volition over time. We were just leaves that knew

how to breathe and we were just animals that had teeth
we could use. And, having teeth did not imply that we
were destined to be hunters or that we were born to roar.

But these who dined before me may have been roar-
ing or they may have been dancing bears, waiting to tame
their dreams.

Acknowledgments

The author wishes to thank Mike Lindgren and the staff at Melville House for the immense love and support. Especially to Mike who often sends the author apt football cards of Kansas City Chiefs QB Patrick Mahomes, along with his own sharp minimalist drawings that never fail to brighten the author's day.

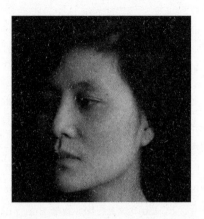

VI KHI NAO was born in Long Khánh, Vietnam, and immigrated to the United States at a young age. Her work includes poetry, fiction, film, and cross-genre collaboration, and has been featured in periodicals such as *Conjunctions*, *The Los Angeles Review of Books*, *Chicago Review*, *Glimmer Train*, *The Baffler*, and *McSweeney's*, and in *The Best American Nonrequired Reading* anthology. A former Black Mountain Institute fellow, she lives in Iowa City.